CROSSROADS
ENCOUNTERS

CROSSROADS ENCOUNTERS

STORIES BY
FREDERICK FOOTE

TABLE OF CONTENTS

Dedicated to:
Helen Boyd, 1928 - 2012
Jarvis Savage, 1946 - 2014

CROSSROADS

The Crossroads is a legendary location in African-American folklore where roads running north-south and east-west cross. At these rural Crossroads, one can meet the devil at midnight and engage in unholy transactions. The usual terms are the seller offers his or her soul in exchange for wealth, fame, beauty, success, etc.

The Crossroads is located in the south in Mississippi or Alabama or anywhere there are country Crossroads and believers.

•

She sits at the Crossroads with her legs akimbo, her dusty brogans facing north and south. Her well-worn plaid skirt and man's blue work shirt are faded and comfortable. The woman's blue denim jacket is threadbare at the elbows and missing an original button, with an odd-shaped ivory replacement.

Her skin is red as Georgia clay and her curly reddish-brown hair is pulled back into a shoulder-length ponytail. She has generous lips, large, too white teeth, a round bump of a nose, and a face disposed to open smiles and loud laughter.

There is a silver mouth harp in her right hand and a long slender joint in her left. She inhales, holds it, closes her eyes, and slowly releases the imprisoned smoke.

By the time she looks south at the dust rising from a car approaching at speed, the joint is ashes. The expensive foreign car slows as it approaches her. It idles to a stop in front of her, the tinted windows reflecting the lowering sun.

The car stands silent, shiny, and black. The dust settles, and it is quieter than before the coupe arrived.

She can almost make out her dusty reflection in the shiny door as she starts to play a slow blues song full of still born things — ripped guts, dark days, regrets and bitterness. Her music is her voice, the still air and parched ground welcome and soak up her wounded words.

The window on the passenger side rolls down, the music invades the dark interior, makes a U-turn and returns to the welcoming dryness of air and earth.

"How much?" The voice is deep, dark, demanding.

She plays a sweet bridge and ups the tempo a little.

"Bitch, you hear me. How much do you want to rent and rend those well-used holes between your dusty, red legs? He won't want your shopworn goods."

She bends notes in an impossible manner.

"I'm being nice. Nicer than he will ever be." He pauses for her response. She plays a not interested, move on blues.

"Bitch, I can get out of this car and take what I want. I will leave you sprawled out, naked and bleeding."

She catches the rhythm, mood, and pitch of his voice and plays his words back to him.

"Are you mocking me? You black, red-faced cunt! You… "

She makes his words sound like a stuck, squealing piglet.

There are the sounds of something pounding and pounding from the insides of the dark space of the car. The car rocks and shudders and finally settles to a standstill.

"I know you're waiting for him. Stupid bitch. He doesn't deal with poor, nigger shit like you. He will fucking destroy you. Fucking stupid cunt!" The voice is tense now with a trace of fear, a little trembling. "Yeah, you wait your stupid black ass here. You'll see."

The mouth harp blasts a train whistle, the chug, chug of a steam locomotive pulling out of the station: traveling music.

The window goes up. The car accelerates without his consent, it spins up a dust storm as it fishtails down the road.

The shadows are long, and the air is cooling as the south bound black-and-white pulls across the road and parks in front of her. There is the chatter of the car radio as the police officer gets out and puts on her campaign hat, tilted forward, shading the black wrap-around sunglasses.

The patrol woman parks her spit-shined boots right in front of the harp player. She stands there silently, staring down as the musician smiles up at her.

"Show me some ID," her voice is thick as molasses and tired as death, with just a suggestion of unreasonable anger barely caged. "Are you another Crossroads groupie?"

She shrugs and opens her arms to show she has no purse. She pats the pockets of her jacket to show they are empty.

"You're messing with me. You're trying to piss me off at the end of my shift." She leans down to the still smiling woman, "ID or go to jail until we ID you, groupie. Your choice."

The harmonica player hits a mournful riff, with a facial expression to match.

The quick kick of the booted foot catches her hard in the shoulder and topples her over backward. The next kick catches her in the right side and lifts her off the ground.

The right foot is raised for another blow when the red-skinned woman plays a shrieking note of rage and the car radio responds with an answering squelch: a burst of angry static ending with a cry of anguish.

The heavy, black boot pauses in midair as the patrol woman turns toward her car in disbelief.

The woman scrambles back away from the cop and plays a sound like leathery wings on a black night, flapping in obscene sensuality.

The radio gasps, stutters and screams, and screams until the sound is painful to the ear and punishing to the soul.

The officer is covering her ears as she falls to her knees. "You, you your kind. These fucking Crossroads… He's not real… just superstition." She fumbles for her gun. The pitch changes, blood gushes from her nose. She bites her tongue, more blood. She turns slowly and crawls toward her car. With each inch the noise eases back, less shrill, less painful.

She crawls into the silent car, loses consciousness for a minute or two.

The musician stands on the shoulder of the road holding her ribs on her right side as the bloody officer straps on her seat belt. Still shaking, the cop starts the car. She accelerates quickly and spins around in a circle and aims the patrol car at the harp woman.

The public address loud speaker, the car radio, and the sirens all explode in sonic madness as the car sweeps by inches from the woman bent in pain, playing her heart out.

The black-and-white calliope rolls into and out of the ditch, through a barbed wire fence and across a field accelerating and accelerating as it carries away the din.

As darkness descends and the night enfolds the land they come from all directions to the Crossroads to sell, trade, and bargain but not with him. He is a myth. They come to dance to her tune in the dark of night.

OUT OF ORDER

Amond flies to his younger brother's bedside without delay. Balter has hours left to live.

Amond's whisked from the station to his brother's estate by private car, family members meet Amond at the door with many thanks and warm embraces.

Amond is shuttled into Balter's bed chambers. His brother, pale and frail, greets him with a heroic effort at good cheer and a shadow of a hearty welcome. Balter is exhausted by his efforts.

They prepare a bath for Amond and provide comely servants to bathe him and attend to his every need.

Amond is oiled and scented, his hair prepared and braided. He is dressed in new linens.

In the great dining hall, the visiting brother is seated at the head of the table. Balter reclines at the foot of the table, barely alive.

All the family is in hushed attendance at this last supper.

They serve the visitor first with Balter's favorite soup. All eyes are on Amond as he tastes the rich steaming chowder.

The spoon drops from his hand. His tongue is seared. His throat constricts. He has been poisoned. "Why?" Is his last word.

Balter responds in a deathly croak, "To put things in order. To let the oldest go first, to usurp this unnatural progression to the grave."

The last word Amond hears is amen.

ROCKET EIGHTY-EIGHT BLUES

I'm slip sliding down the Hell Bound Highway, gliding on my own stinking shit and their warm, slimy blood. Accelerating headlong into the end game, the final round up, the bottom line, the show down.

Showdown at the Rocket 88 Lounge Bar and Grill. Aptly named, a fucking rocket to oblivion fueled by booze, drugs, high-octane self-pity, grand delusions, and good old-fashioned Christian greed along with some battery-acid-strong jealousy. I was made for this place that will bar none and grill your very soul for a joke or just to pass the time of day.

This lizard lounge was made for me. A match made in hell like me and sloe-eyed, luscious-lipped, thick-legged, long-tongue Regina: the Queen of backstabbing, front fucking, and cock sucking. A whore with a heart of stone and mind for gold — a perfect match, I thought.

"I thought," famous fucking last words of fools, philosophers, and children under the age of eight — no, seven — no, five — maybe five. I thought we had a deal, an agreement, a partnership, a fucking contract written in blood, cum, piss and shit.

Yeah, she was dealing, double dealing from the bottom of the deck with hidden, secret, silent partner agreements and a contract. A contract on me. Fuck me!

That's how it started. She fucked me and did it well — so well that I studied her, watched her, checked her out, looked up her resume and pondered her Curriculum Vitae.

Checked it out, up, down and around and it all checked out: molested by father and brother as a child, with an excellent education in elementary sexual deviancy in some of the most highly rated, state certified foster and group homes, and university-level study at two highly regarded state-run institutions of unlikely rehabilitation and certain dehumanization.

What was there not to like with her un-rehabilitated, firm ass, inhumanly proud tits, educated hips and pouting lips?

"So you want me to fuck this nerd motherfucker like this?" She's on top of me with her highly sophisticated pussy working my dick, sucking, and releasing. Bringing me to the edge of heaven on earth, toward that nirvana, that fucking perfect place, that high which acid and coke and heroin can't even pretend to be. Dropping me back, back down, down into ordinary, everyday, pay-by-the-hour fucking. Skyrocketing me back to the edge — up, up and crashing down. Then, finally, explosive peace and death and communion with god knows what.

Back from that sacred place, back to that cheap motel bed and her smile like Mona Lisa, like a Cheshire cat, like the Queen of the 88, like she might start me all over again with her mouth and suck my life down her smooth throat.

"No, no hell, no. Better than that. Blow his fucking mind up. Make him believe your pussy is his only salvation, the cure for all his ills and his only respite in this wicked, wicked world."

She licks her lips with that long tentacle of a tongue, laughs at me with white as death teeth and leans down to whisper in my ear. That tongue to dance in my ear and out my nose and back down my throat and peek out of the head of my dick. That tongue. "Miles, sweet and gentle Miles, fucking like that would kill him and even drive you stark raving, shit-house-rat crazy."

I tremble under the dominion of that tongue.

She puffs her words in my ear like warm, soft clouds, "You do your part. I will part my legs, pucker my lips and move my hips. You won't have anything to complain about." She seals the deal with that same tongue, lips and hips. She makes a believer of me, again. Believing and thinking, thinking and believing, and believing that you are thinking, and thinking that you are believing — that bogus, misleading bullshit fucks you up every time. Every fucking time! I believed she would do her job. I thought I had it all figured out. I believed I was smarter than her high IQ pussy and college-educated tongue, and I thought she believed that too.

One million-five-hundred-thirty-seven dollars and sixty-two cents: I believed that this was the right number, the correct amount, the secret cipher, the winning ticket. I thought I could use this crass cash to create the situations to get the things money can't buy.

The nerd she was fucking so deep and well knew nothing, nothing at all – but his mosey, little, pale girlfriend from Burger King, aahh her brother was the master blaster of hackers.

A loving brother who helps out his now scorned, jilted and dropped without courtesy or consideration little sister in her moment of need making it look like the nerd misdirected the $1,500,037.62. Burger King Girls' share. Nothing more than sweet and sour revenge served like icing on a twenty-year sentence for the nerd. Her brother's share, the love and admiration a sister has for a brother. The Queen of the 88's share, $1,000, easy money for her and a big, but short lived, thrill of a lifetime for the nerd. Everybody gets paid.

My share, well I, I have expenses, and I have bills and I have obligations, but I do OK. I do all right. Except, except there's a tail on me, local scum, thick-faced thugs, bottom-feeders, mouth-breathers, leg-breakers. I can't pick up the money because they will pick me up and put me down hard in a cold place.

They're impatient. They're moving in on me. They'll make me pick up the money or find a way to pick it up themselves. I could run. That's the smart move. I love smart moves. That's the thinking man's answer if you believe that thinking is the answer.

I'm giving up on thinking. I shoot the big one in the eye and the little one, the most dangerous one, in the knee. Not my game this shooting thing. It's a dumb game with no finesse or taste, just brutal. Not a thinking man's game at all.

She's not a thinking man. Not a runner, not a hider — no, not at all. At the bar, at the Lounge, at the 88, knows I'm coming. Watches me in the mirror behind the bar as I slide in on the blood of the big one and the pain of the dangerous one, smiles at me. She does smile at me.

Smiles that promise, that rocket ride to oblivion and beyond. In the 88 with her 38 and my 308, we mate. Stalemate. I ask a gasping gut shot, "Why?" She has a blood bubble breath answer, "You tried to play me and play me cheap... I don't believe... you thought it through."

I SAW THE DEVIL

I'm not a believer. I don't deny the existence of God. I just don't know. In the black community that makes me something of a pariah. It's tough to live like that, but I do.

On the other hand, I have read the Bible at least ten times. I love reading the Bible — the King James Version — but I don't believe a word of it. I don't share my opinion of the Bible with many of my black friends, I need my few remaining friends. I got no time at all for devils and demons and that nonsense.

It's ten A.M. and it's already 101 degrees, the fifth straight day of one-hundred-plus degree heat.

I'm checking my Agapanthus along the driveway. I crack open the side gate to make sure Jake, my 100 pound, red Doberman, has plenty of water. I have my hand on the gate to block Jake from rushing out into the front yard when I feel this wave of fear hit me like a blizzard to the brain. I freeze in the triple digit heat.

Jake hits the gate like a bull out of a rodeo chute, he knocks the gate right out of my hand. He's making a noise, not a fighting noise or his cat killing noise, something else deep and fierce — ugly and disturbing.

Jake charges straight toward the street but there's nothing there.

I glance down the street and coming down the middle of it is a brother as black as the grave: tall, too tall, dressed in a suit the color of midnight madness that's even darker than he is. The suit jacket's draped over his right arm. His shirt's as white and as bright as new fallen snow on a bright day. The suit and shirt are in such sharp contrast that I have to look away. I look at him out of the corner of my trembling eye.

His feet must be size 18 and his shoes are shining like onyx, just like his bald head. He is covering half a block with each step. Fucking impossible!

Jake's headed to where the man will be on his next step.

The man arrives and Jake leaps.

The thing doesn't break stride or turn its head — he glances at Jake, a slight, side-long glance.

Jake crumples like he hit a brick wall at full speed. The impact knocks a brilliant squeal of anguish, a heartbreaking sound, from my dog. Jake hits the ground and claws his way back, dragging his useless back half across the scorching, black, asphalt. Whimpering and shaking, moving as fast as he can, leaving a trail of hot shit to mix with the hot tar of the melting street.

I know it's going to glance at me. I squeeze my eyes shut so tight my eyelids hurt.

I make my fist so hard my muscles knot up.

My vise jaws splinter my teeth.

A concussive wave knocks me on my ass. There is a soft squishing sound as I fall onto the driveway with my eyes still sealed shut.

I crawl into the backyard and I don't open my eyes until I have closed the gate.

I clean up in the backyard, put my soiled clothes in a garbage bag and the bag in the garbage can. I wash off with the garden hose.

I go in, take a forever-shower, sit on the shower floor washing away my tears.

I go check on Jake. He won't come out of his dog house. I pull him out by the collar. His back legs are OK now. He can stand and walk, but he just shakes like he got distemper or something.

And his eyes are hard boiled gray, blind. My dog is blind.

I go in. I lock all my doors and windows, close my blinds and drapes.

I go to the back bedroom, the one farthest from the street. I turn on all the lights. I sit there with my Bible: the one I don't believe a word of. I pray to Him I Have Doubts About to keep me awake. I know if I sleep, that thing, the devil, will open my eyes and his glance will fall on me. I'll look into its eyes. It will be the last thing I ever see.

16

DIOGENES

The heavy, humid days of Omaha are taking their toll on me. I have lost my sea legs for high humidity and seething heat.

A police car rockets by me — sirens blasting and lights flashing — as I pull into the hotel entrance. Something is happening a block north of the hotel. An ambulance races past me, a burst of noise and a blur of flaring lights, as I give the valet the keys to my rental car.

It's 4:00 P.M. and I take refuge in the cool dark of The Lantern, a bar across the street from my lodging. I order a local draft beer and motion for the bartender to give the only other customer: a tired-looking, forty-something bottle blonde, another of whatever she is drinking; and to pour himself one.

I move away from the blonde and the bar to a far table to enjoy the cold beer and the cool solitude of the bar. It is almost a bit of heaven until I look up, and the junkie-thin blonde is standing at my table.

She is what we call PWT or "poor white trash" back in Sumter or "trailer trash" up in Richmond. Her face is tired and old before its time, with bags under her bloodshot, skittish brown eyes, which complement her crow's feet and wrinkled forehead. She may be thirty-five or fifty.

Her drink is in her bony hand and a pleading look is on her narrow face. I should just tell her I'm not interested and send her on her way, but there is in her an air of desperation... a hint of fear. I have seen it too often before. I motion for her to sit. She sits quickly with a thankful sigh.

I reach across the table to shake her hand. "Hi, I'm Ray." She looks confused as if shaking hands was a kind of odd and perverse ritual. The woman offers her hand hesitantly, and I take it gently. She's quaking with fear; it vibrates from her cold hand and up my arm. Now, she is squeezing my hand — holding on for dear life. I try to warm her hand with both of mine.

Her eyes are closed and tears are racing down the sharp angles of her cheeks. We sit like that for a minute or two. I don't have the words to reassure her or comfort her, I only have the touch of my hands.

She finally sobs out an introduction, "I'm… I'm… My name is Trudy. Thank you. Thank you." Trudy reluctantly releases my hand to pull a crumpled tissue from her small purse and tries to dam the flood from her eyes and stop her now dripping nose.

"Trudy, god, I have never met a Trudy. Now you have made my day special."

Trudy tries to laugh, but it comes out like sharp little barks. Her attempt at a smile shows her crooked tobacco stained front teeth. And now, I'm sorry I even came into this bar or to this town. I think this might be more than I want to handle today or any day.

"I think my mama had it in for me from the get go. 'Trudy,' she had to hate me to name me Trudy." She sniffs and dabs at her eyes. "I changed it to Judy in the first-grade… but it was already too late. They called me Trudy-Judy."

Now she laughs a real laugh like she is blowing all the disappointment, debris and dirt out of her life. I laugh with her.

She touches my hand again and leaves her hand on top of mine.

"I'm a mess. I'm sorry… I just… Ray. It is Ray? What do you do? You're not from here, from Omaha."

I pull out a business card. A fancy, high-tech one with my picture in the right-hand corner. When you look at the card from a different angle, you see our company logo where my picture was both in vivid color and 3D.

Trudy-Judy is delighted by the card and holds it at different angles trying to see my picture and the logo at the same time.

"I almost can see both of them. I almost can." She is as happy as a child on Christmas morning.

"Wow, Mr. Raymond Allen, Chief of Performance Evaluation Division, you must be living in high cotton to have such a fancy card and title and all." The laughter leaves her voice, and she is leaning into me with

18

big serious eyes, "Mr. Allen you're a kind man, I see that. But, Mr. Allen, are you a good man?"

The question and the mood change catches me off guard. I bend forward to look deeper into her eyes. I'm looking for something important, but I don't know what it is.

It's disturbing in there, in her eyes. I look away, blink and wonder. I think about the question. I don't owe her any answers, we both know that. I also know I have to answer this question, not for her but for me.

We sit in silence. The bartender brings us new drinks on the house.

She sips and watches and waits.

I take a long swallow of my beer. I steel myself, focus trying to get the right words, to get the words right.

"I'm not so kind. I'm not the kind of person you think I am." She is concentrating on me one-hundred percent now. "If I've done some good things, it's been by accident."

I stand up. I finish my beer and look around the bar. I look down at her.

"I'm not a good man." I look into those dangerous eyes. "I'm not going to heaven, Trudy. I might even get rejected in hell."

I sink back into my chair. I'm exhausted. "I think I'm going to call it a day. Nice meeting you, Trudy."

I settle up with the bartender.

When I step out into the swamp outside, Trudy is waiting for me.

"Mr. Allen, I need a place to stay for an hour or so and to be with someone. I need it in the worst way."

The fear is there in her, but she tries to control it.

I'm as tired as I have ever been. I don't need company right now. I don't need this needy, seedy, dangerous Trudy company ever.

But, she touches me deeply, reminds me of someone or something. I offer her my arm and we go up to my hotel room.

•

I have a suite with a kind of sitting room with a comfortable leather couch and a big, easy chair. Trudy's shivering as she falls onto the couch rubbing her arms to restore warmth. I turn up the thermostat, grab a blanket and place it around her shoulders.

"Trudy, do you need a doctor? The hotel…"

She cuts me off and motions toward the mini bar. I collect two miniature scotch bottles and sit beside her with my arm around her shoulders.

Trudy drinks the scotch in a quick swallow. I place my bottle in her trembling hands.

Slowly, the shaking subsides. She looks up at me. "Mr. Allen, what…"

"Call me Ray. Mr. Allen is my father."

"What did you do so bad? Did you do it for power or money?" Her voice is shaky and slurred.

I look around my comfortable room from the vantage point of my good life without want or scarcity. She has closed her eyes. There is the hum of the heating unit and the sound of a door closing in the hallway.

"Acts of kindness… of a sort… I thought they were… I did it, I did it for love of beauty or to pass the time… I'm not so sure anymore."

Her breathing is soft and regular, and her face is relaxing. I feel at peace.

"Was it worth it?" It is a soft whisper of a question.

My answer is even softer. "I don't know. I'll know when my bill comes due."

Now she reaches out and takes my hand to comfort me this time.

●

There is a loud, persistent pounding on my hotel door. It wakes me, leaves me disoriented. Trudy is gone. I'm still on the couch. The blanket is over me. It is still daylight.

I stumble to the door and open it to find two cops, detectives probably, in street clothes. One a tall stoop shouldered man in his forties with an aggressive beak of a nose bookended by kind eyes.

The other one is shorter, with a big belly and a stout build. He has mean little pig eyes in a round face.

"Mr. Raymond Allen?"

I nod yes.

"I'm Detective Sherpa and this is Detective Wintersmith. Do you have a minute to assist us in an investigation?"

Sherpa has a nice baritone voice, well-modulated like he has stage or public speaking experience.

"About what? What time is it?"

"We need to talk to you in private, Allen, not in the fucking hallway. We won't take much of your precious time."

I turn to look at Wintersmith. He stares back at me with the same irritation on his face as he had in his voice. "Detective Wintersmith, you will not take up any of my time, precious or otherwise. Good day, detectives."

I start to close the door.

"Wait, wait just a minute. There has been an accident."

"Detective Sherpa, I don't engage in conversations where I'm kept ignorant of the nature of the discussion."

"We can do this downtown, Allen. Get your coat."

"Only if you have a warrant or reasonable suspicion and even then I will only talk when I have an attorney present."

Now Wintersmith is in the winter of his discontent. His cheeks and nose are as red as Christmas berries. He is clenching and unclenching his hands in frustration.

Sherpa calls up his soothing baritone, "No, no need for that." He pulls a picture from his jacket pocket and holds it out in front of me. "Do you recognize…"

It is an enlarged driver's license photo of Trudy with red hair and less luggage under her eyes and fewer lines in her face.

I push my door closed.

The baritone booms through my door, "Mr. Allen, I think you recognize her. Mr. Allen, she's dead."

There is quiet in the hallway as if the whole floor is waiting for my response. Even the AC is holding its breath.

I open the door, let them in. I grab another scotch and sit uneasy in my easy chair. I glance at the time on the clock radio, it is 10:10. I can't recall ever having slept so long before or so well.

Sherpa sits on the end of the couch next to my chair. He removes a clear plastic evidence bag from his jacket pocket with my business card in it. "She was holding this in her hand when she died, we had to wait until your San Diego office opened to find you. How well did you know her?"

I sip my scotch and try to understand how well I knew her. Sherpa is patient, but Wintersmith is in a rude rush.

"Was it a professional relationship, Allen? She was a pro."

I turn back to Sherpa. "I met her yesterday. I just knew her name. That's about all I know."

"Did you give her the business card?" I nod yes to Sherpa.

"When did you meet her, Mr. Allen?" Sherpa has a notepad and pen out now as he waits for me to answer his question.

Wintersmith wades into the interlude between question and answer, "Did you know her in the biblical manner or was she too washed up for a high roller like you?"

"I met her in The Lantern, the bar across the street, about ... a little after four."

Both officers come to point like bird dogs. They are pointing at me. They exchange looks, and both turn back to me with greater intensity.

"Mr. Allen, you say you met Wilma Street, the victim, a little after 4:00 P.M. yesterday?"

"No, I didn't say that. I met the woman whose picture you showed me at The Lantern at a little after four. She said her name was Trudy. What's the problem?"

"Allen, where were you just before you met the victim?"

I turn to answer Wintersmith. "I was outside the entrance of this hotel giving my car to the parking valet."

"Which valet? Do you remember?"

I think a minute before responding to Wintersmith's question.

"White, male about six-foot tall, brown hair, brown eyes, light beard... Al, Albert, Alec — his name is Alec."

Baritone takes his turn. "Was there anything out of the ordinary going on when you were there with Alec?"

"Not really. No, wait, there was a police car and an ambulance full of lights and sounds racing up the street to an incident a block north of the hotel."

Sherpa flips through his note pad. "Mr. Allen, at 3:50 P.M. a doctor from this very hotel declared Wilma Street dead at the scene of the accident you noticed."

They are leaning toward me waiting for a response. I let them wait until Wintersmith starts fidgeting and making fists again. I let him get his mouth open before I speak.

"Maybe I'm mistaken, perhaps I met someone else. You could check with the bartender on duty last night at The Lantern or the hallway and lobby cameras."

Sherpa is quick off the mark. "Mr. Allen, are you speaking of the hotel's cameras?"

"The very same. Trudy spent some time with me here in this room."

"I bet she did, Allen. You fucking lied to me. I asked…"

"There was no sex, Wintergreen. No money changed hands, sorry to disappoint you."

"Then what the fuck was she doing up here in your room?"

I turn back to Sherpa. "Apparently, there is an identification problem. Let's talk again when that issue is resolved." I stand, cross to and open my door.

Wintergreen turns on me snarling, "Bullshit, asshole, you can't…"

Sherpa's phone rings. He raises his hand to silence his partner. "Mr. Allen, would you give me just a minute? I might have some insight into the identification confusion."

We both watch Sherpa as he goes through a series of yes and no responses. He concludes his conversation and fusses with his phone for a minute.

"Records has sent me the file based on Mrs. Street's fingerprints." He consults his phone. "The dead woman was using Wilma Street's ID. The prints belong to a Trudy May Anderson, born in Mobile, Alabama thirty-five years ago. She has an extensive record of prostitution, theft, embezzlement, fraud, possession, and blackmail: all before she was twenty." Sherpa pauses, and his stare grows sharp as he looks at me. "Her young, but impressive criminal career ends suddenly after she is released on bail from her arrest. I'm waiting on her booking photo."

I shrug. I shake my head. "Well, that is interesting. We still have the problem of me meeting with a dead woman though, so if you will excuse me I have a conference call I have to take in ten minutes." My cell phone rings. It is my office. I usher the officers out. Sherpa gives me his business card and Wintergreen gives me threatening looks.

I can't even get to the bathroom. There are major unforeseen issues with our conference call. One hour and ten-minutes later, all is well in the Performance Evaluation Division again.

As I dash toward the bathroom, there is an impatient knock on my door that sounds unwelcomely familiar.

It is the two detectives. They look a bit disturbed and as always Wintergreen is angry.

Wintergreen pushes his way into my room. "What the fuck are you trying to pull asshole? Do you think we're all stupid in the Midwest? I'm about to arrest your California ass on GP."

"Mr. Allen, we do have a problem. Would you just sit for a moment and see if we can make sense of this... confusion?"

I nod at Sherpa as I settle into my easy chair. Sherpa returns to his former place on the couch. Wintergreen moves behind my chair out of my vision.

"We talked to Fields, the bartender, and he confirms that you were in the bar with a woman at the time you said you were. And the hotel cameras and staff confirms that you brought that same woman to this room."

I wait for the punch line. They wait for me to respond. It's a standoff.

Finally, Sherpa removes his phone and makes some adjustments and hands me the phone. There is a picture of a very attractive dark-haired girl about nineteen or twenty years of age. The very type of woman who fascinates me in the extreme. She is the perfect age for me. I find her irresistible. I stare for far too long. I flick the picture and there are shots of me and that beautiful girl approaching my room. I keep flicking through the pictures, back and forth, back and forth. I know who she is. Her name was Ashley when I met her. I should have recognized her when I met her in The Lantern. She was my first one. My first true love. How could I not recognize her even in a different body?

I reluctantly return the phone.

"Mr. Allen, do you know who this woman is?"

I nod yes. "Detective Sherpa, do you know who she is?"

The detective looks distinctly uncomfortable. He stares out the window and looks up at his partner. He works his phone for a minute and hands me back the phone.

"She, the woman you were with, bears an uncanny resemblance to Trudy May Anderson at age nineteen."

There is a mug shot of Trudy at nineteen. Her beauty turns the mug shot into a work of art.

"Why did you lie to us about how she looks? I mean that was stupid."

I don't turn around to respond to Wintergreen. I keep my eyes on Sherpa.

"You didn't lie, did you? You told the truth about what you saw."

I acknowledge the accuracy of Sherpa's statement with another nod.

"Mr. Allen, whoever she is, we saw pictures of her coming to your room and entering your room, but none of her leaving this room."

Ashley was number one. There have been fifteen since. I know where Ashley is and how she is. She's in my bathtub in this hotel room with her head; arms and legs removed, and her limbs severed at the major joints. Every cut executed with gentle affection. Her head, beautifully coffered hair and exquisitely made-up face, rest on her chest with her eyes open and looking out in loving wonderment.

I didn't do it this time… I gave her sweet repose fifteen years ago… or maybe I did it again. I don't know. It doesn't matter anyway. I loved them, each and all. I showed them every kindness possible.

I wonder whether Sherpa will grant me the small kindness to use the bathroom before they arrest me. My bladder is about to burst.

WIND SONG

He was born in the Acorn Forest during the harvest season, a young mother's first.

The slight breeze slipped into the hut through cracks, crevices, under blankets and down smoke holes. She licked at the birth membrane, tasted the blood and caressed the damp, brown skin.

Her tender breath touched him at the same time as the midwife. The mild current claimed him, chained him, bound him to her.

The gentle wind stroked his cheek, ruffled his hair, breathed softly up his nose, whisked away his breath, and whispered in his ears: all expressions of her airy, loving affection.

On his mother's back, in the swinging cradle, or on the buffalo blanket, she teased him with feathers, bits of grass, leaves, danced them in front of him in and out of reach. She twisted and turned in delight at his every smile and soared with his every laugh.

He named her "Play," claimed her with smiles, bound her with joyous laughter. She was his favorite playmate, his constant companion, protector, and teacher.

Play would sing to him in the rustle of leaves and grass, talk to him in whistles and sighs.

At a certain age his mother admonished and astonished him. She directed him to put Play aside: "Son of mine. Sunshine of my days. It is time to put away the companions of youth and heed the attractions of the willowy, shy girls; the laughing, brown-eyed girls; and girls of clever hands and sweet affections."

And he did. He did court and escort bright-eyed girls with good teeth; and stout girls with warm thighs; and girls with honey mouths and sweet berry tongues.

And Play laughed and promised him better than that assortment of youth, desire, and fertility could ever provide.

Playfully she slipped under his clothes and tickled and teased with a warm touch and excited him in untold ways.

Play crushed the berries and winged the juice to his waiting lips and rocked his ever-ready hips and came to him in secret in his hours of desire.

The pleasing breeze coated herself with honey for his delight and denied him no pleasure in her competence.

Still, a thin, dark-skinned, dark-eyed girl with a bell of a laugh pulled, tugged, lured and demanded his attention and affection. The thin one insisted with the tilt of a hip or the curve of a lip or a casual glance.

The dark-eyed girl slipped into his dreams and his thoughts as easily as Play slipped into his dwellings and clothes.

Play was stormy. She scolded, chided, nagged, promised and cajoled. He smiled at her. Sung to her. Told her the stories she loved, but, but his time with Play dwindled to too little to count.

He did not count on her rage. Play came now as a hot furnace blast from the desert and scorched the crops and stirred the dry soil to rebellion. Dust and grit were her emissaries and invaded the food, the drink, the beds and the baths.

The unending heat, dust, and grit with relentless, blistering winds drove some mad, or deep into despair, or to a different place.

Except, the misery bound him and thin, dark-eyes tighter and tighter, so tight they were married without benefit of ceremony or notice.

Devoid of play, Play erupted.

He reasoned with unreasonable Play.

The thin girl bulged in the middle and smiled more than ever.

Now a hurricane, Play ripped the camp to shreds and scattered the pieces too far ever to be recovered. She smiled on her works and found them pleasing.

He begged her to cease.

Play ignored him.

The thin girl blossomed.

His mother came again, to save their tribe: "Son of mine, bringer of unending nights of winged wretchedness you are our curse and cure. Time now for a cure."

He groveled, pleaded, entreated and prayed to Play. She beat him with heavy blows and scalded him and froze him and scrubbed his skin raw. Humorless Play would not relent one whit.

The tribe banished him, and his not-so-thin-now wife would not leave him. His mother gave them scraps and bits and pieces, more than she could spare.

The not-so-thin-now girl's mother gave the same, all damp with tears.

Fierce Play pelted them with splintered sticks and jagged stones, sliced at them with icy talons, cursed them with her fiery breath, herded them to the barren wastelands and echoing canyons. She denied them haven or shelter, rest or respite.

He shielded his wife from her outrage as best he could and offered himself to Play as slave or servant or sacrifice if only she allowed his near-death wife life.

On that rocky ledge, Play saw in the not-so-skinny-girl a second chance, a new young one to please, and tease and raise right this time. Play relented, regretted, shined with remorse and begged forgiveness. Her touch was gentle, soothing, healing and warm. She embraced and held them both in her protection.

Such as it was. Play's mother arrived, as a wind undeniable and unstoppable. She swept the battered couple up and smashed them down, down into the rock walls. Shredded and ripped them asunder and scattered the skin, bones, flesh and hair beyond recovery.

"Child of mine, delight of my days, it is time to put away the companions of youth and give over to the attentions of the sly gusts, gentle breezes, zesty zephyrs and fierce gales."

And Play did as her mother commanded, with only a wispy ache of longing.

COURT-MARTIAL OF SAMUEL JAMES WILSON

"All right, Captain Clay, it's your turn to drink from the bitter cup. You need to weave your peculiar brand of Southern gothic magic and turn this acerbic cup into a wine that'll astonish the palate and amaze the mind. You do understand me?"

I'm standing at attention. I'm the only JAG in the Office that's required to stand at attention like this. This Yankee colonel has a distinct bias against everything southern.

"Sir…"

The uncouth three-hundred pound polar bear in an Army uniform belches.

"You have the unparalleled good fortune to represent our most infamous client, Corporal Samuel James Wilson. This is a career maker son — or a heart breaker. Your simple task is to save that young soldier from the noose. You understand that, Tulane?" The Yankee's a graduate of the Yale Law School. How he must despise even the very sight of my lily-white, southern ass.

I'm at attention. I take a deep breath. "Colonel, Sir, if this solider did desert his unit as charged, if he did provide critical intelligence to the enemy that resulted in the devastating defeat at Camp Oswald, and if he was the consort of General Pham, it may be beyond my power to…"

The Colonel comes out of his chair like some great white ICBM launched to bring death and destruction down on me and mine, it's a frightening sight to behold.

"Do you understand your orders, Captain?"

"Sir, I…"

"Captain, do you understand your orders?"

"Yes, Sir. I understand my orders, Sir."

He clenches and unclenches his paws. He looks at me as if I were a new, odd breed of imbecile. He shakes his head in disgust and points to the case files on his desk. I step forward and pick up the files. I stand at attention.

"Do not fuck this up, Southern Comfort, a man's life's at stake here. In the eyes of your southern God of Wrath, Wilson's worth more than the both of us combined. Understand that."

I don't understand that at all. Where did that observation come from? What does it mean?

I escape the Colonel's office with the disturbing idea that God has somehow found us wanting and favors a Negro deserter, coward, and traitor over me.

●

I work better from my quarters than in the office. I start with the pictures in the case file. I let them spill out of their envelopes and folders onto my kitchen table and the floor without order or direction. Some are covered by other pictures. Others are upside down. It doesn't matter. The important ones will reveal themselves. They always do.

God does not favor the Negro corporal. He's going to hang. I know that. The Colonel knows that. God knows that.

I reach down and pick up a picture of a younger, pre-enlistment Wilson. He's standing beside a tiny, gray-haired black woman. She's shooting an ice pick look at me, piercing my eyes, lacerating my heart, stabbing my soul.

I fling the picture away, jump back away from the eyes. I'm shaking and short of breath. I leave the picture on the floor. I dash into my bedroom. My shaking hands remove the picture of me and my grandmother from the frame. I take care to avoid looking into her eyes. I return to the kitchen and use my picture to scoop up that other picture from the floor, put them both in a manila envelope and seal the envelope with my spit. I hide the envelope under my underwear in my dresser. Still shaken, I retreat to my big comfort chair and the brandy is warm and wonderful. After the second one I return to the other pictures.

•

I pick up a letter from an Army intelligence captain from the pile. It explains that there was no open case on Pham, but they have some pictures of her that were taken when investigating other bar girls as possible spies. The captain has circled Pham in these pictures

The picture I pick up is of four bar girls posing in a Negro bar. Two of the girls are ravishing. The third is big-breasted with a pretty face, but not in the same league with the other two. I do not need the circle to recognize Pham. She's tiny, thin, shabbily dressed, poorly presented. She dominates the picture. The girls on either side of her leave ample distance between them and her out of respect. The two girls on Pham's right look in at her to understand how they should behave in this photo. Pham looks straight ahead, into me, sly, intelligent, in control. She's fearless. I do not try to stare her down. I handle the picture with great care.

Another brandy or two. How could Army Intelligence miss her? She has such presence in a picture! How the fuck could they miss her? A spy? Looking for a spy? Stupid fucks! There she was, the commander of the Home Defense Forces in Ha Binh Province, on display with all that power and authority and they were looking for spies. I'm shaking with anger and frustration. She has the same kind of presence and power as the two women in my underwear drawer. How in the world could anyone miss that?

•

The knock on my door takes me by surprise. I check my watch, it's seventeen-thirty hours. I have spent the whole day studying two pictures.

•

The Colonel has summoned me. He asks me how Wilson is holding up. I confess I've not yet visited Wilson.

His voice is kind, his tone is mild.

"Wilson has the whole weight of the United States Army crushing the life from him. He's in a hopeless, hapless position. He's a pariah. He's alone. He might just appreciate contact with the one person in the whole world who's obligated by law and morality to defend him."

The Colonel puts his heavy arm around my shoulder. At that moment I fear for my life at the hands of this mad Colonel. I make it to the stockade in record time.

•

Wilson is dark-chocolate brown with perfect white teeth and an athletic build. He's a handsome man, with a smile that lights up his whole face. I dislike him on sight. No, I disliked him on seeing his picture the first time. No, I disliked him from the first time I heard his name. It's not just that he's a Negro. I grew up in the company of Negroes. For the most part, I found them lazy and unreliable. There are exceptions to every rule that prove the rule. He may or may not be the exception, but I dislike him in a more fundamental way that I find difficult to define.

He takes all this in at a glance. He understands I despise him. He has southern ways in his blood — we are kin. He still smiles at me and offers me his hand. I'm ashamed of myself. I can see, feel my grandmother turning her scorching gaze on me. It makes me hate him even more.

Introductions are over. We sit there in a comfortable silence. We know where we stand. I like it like this. No lies yet. I ask him to tell me his story.

She approached him in a bar. She insulted him. He teased her. Weeks later he saved her from an attack by a Special Forces Sergeant. She was not grateful. He met her again in the company of some of his friends. They spoiled her transaction with a young GI and laughed at her.

He went back to "check on her." He touched her. They were wed at that touch. They "fucked" over the next few months as often as they could until he realized who she was. They "fucked" one last time after that. They "fucked" while the three Northern Provinces were starting to fall and Camp Oswald was being decimated — bad, bad timing. She arranged a car to take him back to an Army controlled area.

They never talked about military issues. She never asked. He never volunteered. They're not in love. It's much stronger than love. We leave it at that.

I report back to the Colonel. It's nineteen-hundred hours. He's still in the office, waiting.

●

I believe him, every word. I know he's going to hang now. The other charges do not matter. He was having carnal knowledge of the author of the destruction of his comrades in arms while they were dying. He'll hang for that. All four charges against him are hanging charges. Even if I succeed in getting one or two dismissed or reduced, which is highly unlikely, he will still hang. He'll not lie about his relationship with her. That'll put the raw rope around his tender neck.

Back in my room I unseal the two photographs. He's standing with his grandmother. I know that without asking. He has his arm around her with his hand on her shoulder. She's uncomfortable with that small show of affection. He knows it. He's teasing her. She's annoyed. They're happy to be with each other. I turn to me and my grandmother. We're standing side by side. We're not touching. We're looking straight ahead. I'm uncomfortable around her. I would never, ever dare tease her.

Both grandmothers are bigger than they appear. They dominate the pictures if you look closely. Both old women ignore me. I'm beneath contempt to them. Fuck them. What can I do? His words and deeds will hang him. Fuck them. I seal them in a new envelope. I hide the envelope in my book case.

●

Our second session is on life at Camp Oswald. Oswald was our most isolated post with two hundred troops and six Airlift troop-cargo copters and a small Cessna for forward observation. The Provincial Capital of Vinh, a town of several thousand, was less than ten miles from the Camp. The 9th Infantry company was there to "secure the Province against enemy incursion and to protect the inhabitants from coercion and exploitation by enemy forces." They carried out their missions with regular patrols and "quick air response to incidents of aggression." This is the purpose of Camp Oswald according to the U.S. Army.

The Corporal has a different view of the Camp. He calls it "Happy Camp" because everyone was happy and high or drunk most of the time.

Patrols did go out on a regular basis, but only to find a quiet, relatively safe spot to get high or sleep off a previous high. The Happy Camp troops and the insurgents took great pains to avoid each other. Happy Camp causalities were low and mostly self-inflicted. The Happy Camp troops were very religious. They prayed to the insurgents to let them come back from each patrol and to let Happy Camp survive another day. Camp security was pretty much a joke. Why pretend to be secure when there was no way in hell you could keep the enemy out or even tell who the enemy was most of the time?

If you weren't on patrol or some other assignment you could leave the camp pretty much at will, just be back in time for your next assignment. The rumor was that the insurgents were providing them with the high quality weed, Green Witch. The Witch was ubiquitous. It was pretty much a live and let live arrangement until the Special Forces showed up and actually wanted to "kill some gooks."

I check it all out. I substantiate each and every one of his claims. The picture is worse than he presented. Happy Camp is a place of despair where men have been abandoned to perform an impossible task. They are hopelessly outnumbered and outgunned by the enemy. Happy Camp exists because the insurgents allow it to exist. Everyone knows Camp Oswald is a bad joke played on the men and officers assigned to the Camp.

•

I have lunch with Corporal Wilson every day. I bring the foods he likes. I pay for the food, but I feel like he's treating me. I want to hear about him and his grandmother. I want to know if she overpowered him, if she ruled the entire family with an iron fist. I always end up talking about me and my grandmother. After each visit I swear I'll not visit him again, but I do. I visit every day. I live for those visits. Am I falling in love with Corporal Wilson or is it something stronger than that?

•

And so the court-martial commences. I do the best work of my life. I exceed even my own high opinion of myself. I get the desertion charge dismissed early on. Four other charges are dismissed over the next three days. The treason charge stands. The prosecution theory is that Wilson told

34

Pham about the plans for a "secret" mass sweep of the northern three provinces, thus enabling the enemy to strike at the optimal time. And that by having intercourse during the attack on Camp Oswald he gave substantial aid and comfort to the enemy. It's all bullshit. Bullshit that will leave him dangling from a rope.

Tomorrow's the last day of the court-martial. I'm amazed. I didn't think I would get any character witnesses for Wilson. I talked to thirteen men who served with him. To a man they're willing to testify on his behalf. Amazing, but he'll still hang.

I'm in the Colonel's office. It's twenty-one-hundred hours. We're drinking scotch straight up. The Colonel is deep into his cups. "Captain, do you see it now? Do you understand political theater?"

I nod. "I'm out of moves, Sir. I… I… I'm sorry." I'm near collapse. This is the hardest I have fought for anything in my entire life.

The Colonel ignores me. "Political theater, we put those tiny little outposts up there so we can claim that we control the Northern Provinces. The American people see the map of our control. It looks like we control most of the damn country."

"Colonel, is there anything at all we can do now? Anything?"

The Colonel is lost in his world of political theater. "The insurgents play along. Once we claim the area is pacified we find it difficult to justify major military actions in these areas or even reinforcements for our boys. The insurgents can move troops and material through at will. It would be suicide for an outpost to take on the insurgents, political theater."

Happy Camp fell so quickly, in part, because General Austen, the Commander of Northern Forces, had implemented a "secret" coordinated mass sweep of the three Northern Provinces, dispersing the troops from four camps and three bases. All these bases and camps fell within a seventy-two hour period. The sweep was a crazy idea to start with, and it was far from secret. I have shown that in the court-martial. It's not enough. I have established that Corporal Wilson did not know about the attacks at the time he had his last sexual encounter with Colonel Pham. It's not enough. He was fucking Colonel Tien Pham while his friends were dying. Tomorrow the court-martial will end. The death watch will start. The colonel has passed out at his desk.

I stagger home. A small brown box is on my doorstep. I open it in my kitchen, pictures. I turn the box over and let the pictures fall to the table. I pick up a picture of General Austen. He's not alone. He's sharing his bed with a very nude, very gorgeous Asian woman. I recognize her instantly as one of the beauties from the bar picture with Pham. I call the colonel. He tells me to ram that picture up their collective asses.

I get the judge and the prosecutor out of bed. We meet at the judge's home. The pictures are examined with considerable intensity. Calls are made. Coffee is consumed. Calls are returned. More coffee is consumed. We wait for one call. It comes at zero-six-hundred hours. Corporal Wilson will plead guilty to a lesser charge and do six years with a dishonourable discharge. I want to run to Wilson and give him the good news. I need to call the colonel, but first... As soon as I get to my quarters I take the envelope out of the bookshelf. The grandmothers are still ignoring me. Fuck them! What more can I do? I toss the pictures on the floor and collapse onto my big living room chair.

I need to see a picture of Wilson and Pham together, now. I dream the picture. She's straddling his lap wearing a tight, short skirt. She's pulling down his zipper. He's ripping off her panties. This is not a show of affection... no... no... it's something else... lust... more... than lust... uncompromising need... I can smell them in heat... disorienting... I think, I have the absurd belief that the War, the whole War, was just an event to bring these two together. I awake suddenly with a sense of alarm. I race to the stockade. Wilson comes in the interview room looking very somber. I want to give him the good news. I want to give him me. He doesn't want to listen or talk. He embraces me, thanks me and tells me to go home. He tells me everything will be all right, but he's not talking about himself. He's talking about me. There's nothing wrong with me. I'm safe. I'm almost sound.

•

The two grandmothers are smiling at me, at me. They look proud. I don't understand why or what happened. Still, I feel better than I can remember feeling in a long time. Something phenomenal has happened somewhere. Something epic and I have been part of it. I know that. I don't think saving Corporal Wilson's life is that event.
I sleep my best sleep in a long time. The last thing I remember is the musky odour of their love making.

WRITER'S CAMP

Oh, I know you. I know the language of your face and the taste of your spit and the smell of your shit. I know you, Kaden, your odd ways and salacious salad days. I know you shamelessly and seamlessly without lapse or omission.

Wyoming. Why the fuck am I driving these table-lands on an October evening, to a place I have never seen for Rika — a mean and cruel, unforgiving bitch who tried to destroy me and mine — body and soul? For the money? Shit, I never even set a price. What the fuck am I doing?

I know how you fuck and suck, and the curve in your dick and the glint in your eyes. I know your secret hungers.

According to the GPS, the Crossroads are two miles ahead and then a right for another three miles along a dirt road that leads to the cabin. The cabin that will be just right for me. Just like Rika said. I fucking despise her to death and beyond. I truly do. She gets under my skin and on my last nerves. But, here I am trying to save her boney-ass, why? Why? That is the fucking question.

Kaden, you want to fuck me now, right now. Don't shake your head don't deny it. Don't lie. Never lie to me about that Kaden. I need you. I need you to save me, yes, to rescue me. Don't cum on yourself with glee. At least try to hide your pleasure in my pain. You name your price. I will even throw in a free fuck or two. Would you like that? Huh? Miyuki will never know unless you tell her. Kaden, don't get angry and don't leave until you hear me out. I won't mention your treacherous Japanese slut again. I promise. Just listen and hear my prayer to you.

Save her? I need someone to save me. Save me from fucking up again. It will be different with Miyuki. It has to be. I need to save me from myself. I... shit! What? There is someone ahead... at the Crossroads... a woman standing out here in the middle of fucking nowhere. A sister! My god. What the fuck. I slow down and pull my rented Beamer over in front of her. She is red like Georgia clay with a smile like the sun on fresh snow. And laughing eyes. Aaahh, shit.

I'm out of the car in a flash. I scoop her up in my arms and swing her around, laughing like a loon. She laughs with me. A glorious, wonderful full-bodied, lusty, honest laugh.

I finally put her down and rest my hands on her shoulders. "My name is Kaden. Who are you? What the hell are you doing out here?"

She puts her hands on my shoulders and grins up at me. "Waiting for you, Mr. White. I'm waiting for you."

"For me? What? How did you know my name?"

She pulls down her hands and slips a harmonica from the pocket of her worn denim jacket and plays like James Cotton — she plays a little Junior Wells and smiles at me again. "You need to get to work, Kaden. I will see you anon. I promise."

"Look, look... waiting for me... that is a delightful line, but it's getting dark and chilly. Do you have a car? How did you get here? Are you alone? Did Rika put you up to this? What..."

"Wow! You have a lot of questions. Are you really glad to see me?"

"You are the first black person I have seen in Wyoming. Yes, I'm glad to see you. Are you real?"

She plays a little Sonny Terry. "Kaden, I have a little business to attend to, OK? Go on and I will see you later if you like."

I stand there in the deepening shadows arguing with her. Telling her I can't leave her alone out here. She plays a little Carey Bell, kisses me on the cheek, and pushes me into the front seat of my car. I give her directions to my cabin.

She is still playing as I drive away.

I'm out of the business, Kaden. They have blacklisted me. Right now, no studio will work with me. My investors have run off or been scared off. Right now, I could not produce a puppet show. I have an amazing property and a gifted director and my own money, but I don't have a screenplay. And you, Kaden, are the script doctor. I need you to give me a script in forty-eight hours.

I didn't even get her name: the red woman, the sister at the Crossroads. The further away from her I get the less real the encounter is. But my last meeting with Rika, that is indelible.

Give me the script I need in forty-eight hours, and I will do anything you ask, pay any price. You will own me. Except, I will not forgive Miyuki — that I cannot do.

And that was the perfect opportunity to tell Rika to kiss my fat, black ass. To leave her there in her designer clothes and thousand-dollar haircut with her immense savagery and boundless anger. I looked at her, into her fierce gray eyes, studied her long face and thin lips. Lips I can still taste. "I don't want to own you, Rika. I want you to leave Miyuki and me the fuck alone. That's what you can do for me, for us. Send me your fucking property." My last words to her.

She knows I write best in isolation — near water and wildlife and big skies. So that's why I'm headed toward a cabin I have never seen to try and save the career of a woman who was my friend and lover and colleague. A woman who tried desperately to destroy me and Miyuki.

I must be fucking crazy.

●

The cabin is perfect — surrounded by bright woods and full of light, feeling warm and natural with a sliding glass door looking out over a stream thirty yards away. There is an Ugly Stick rod, Penn spinning reel, and a tackle box by the door to the rear porch facing the stream. A cottonwood grove to the north and a sprinkling of willows to the south.

I call Miyuki on the satellite phone, there are no cell towers around here. She is short with me, angry that I took this job. She calls right back and apologizes. We talk about our baby's coming birth and life as parents and other odds and ends. I relax, step out on the back porch. I fit in here. I can write here.

Rika has given me a perfect writing camp.

●

I will need every ounce of this perfection. Rika calls on the satellite phone. The property is a short novel, ninety-seven pages, by Ambrosia Anderson: a sister, a schoolmate and mutual friend. Fire Friction is one of my favorite books and it is full of poetry and love and hate and betrayal and redemption in a very devastating and unnatural manner. Difficult, difficult, difficult if not impossible to script.

I reread the novel on my laptop computer on the back porch in the clean, crisp, night air.

There is something I need to do. Someone I need to check on... someone I need.

The knock on my front door comes at 2:00 A.M. I'm eating cheese and salami and drinking a local craft beer.

It's the red sister at my door.

"Kaden, may I come in?"

I pull her through the door and to the table. Her hands are freezing.

"God, woman, you are cold. Coffee? Would you like coffee?"

She laughs her big laugh and hugs me. "Kaden, you are kind and..."

"Sit. Are you hungry?"

She is hungry, cold and exhausted. I feed her and direct her to the smaller of the two bedrooms.

"Kaden, you are kind and generous. Thank you." She kisses me on the cheek, closes the bedroom door, and leaves me to my night work.

•

I wake at noon to the smell of coffee, bacon and sausage, almost on the edge of an idea of how to write this screenplay... just out of reach.

I see her now in the clear light of day. A full face, bright brown eyes and luscious lips — she is about five-six with inviting, easy riding curves.

She serves me, plays the harp for me and gives me the launching pad for the day. I enjoy watching her talk, play, and move. I'm already fond of her.

I put on my hiking boots, hug her goodbye, holding her just a little too long.

I hike north along the creek to clear my mind. Watch and listen and feel. I fall into the landscape, float into the sky.

An hour later, I'm back at the cabin. The red woman is gone. The kitchen is immaculate. There is a note: "Kaden, thank you. Could I impose on you tonight again? It will be appreciated."

I take a beer and my computer onto the back porch. I use the phone hotspot function to check my email. A fish jumps in the creek.

I write.

Lately, I make my living rewriting scripts, screenplays, even video scripts on short notice. Rika wrecked my regular employment opportunities. Speed is my specialty. I may get three to five jobs a year. Last year I worked less than thirty-days. But, I get paid. I still don't believe how much I get paid.

I work from 4:30 P.M. to 4:00 A.M. I barely notice the red woman come in and make fresh coffee, eat and kiss me on the cheek.

It is done all in one draft. I have done the impossible. It is the best thing I have ever written. I close up my computer, put on my jacket and boots, step out into the night air.

I walk a few yards from the cabin, and I fall to my knees weeping uncontrollably. I give prayers of thanksgiving for my creation, for the words that will bring this story into a new life on the screen.

I call Rika at 6:00 A.M. I email her the screenplay which is more script than screenplay.

I pace around waiting for her response.

At 7:00 in the morning, the phone rings. I answer immediately. There is silence. "Hello, hello… Rika?"

"Kaden Whistler White, I love it." There is a long silence. "Thank you, thank you, Kaden."

While Rika is setting up a conference call to Ambrosia, I call Miyuki and send her the script.

I pace again. Miyuki is the real writer with published novels and poetry and awards and recognition. Her opinion means everything to me.

She is crying when she calls back, tears of joy.

There is no conference call. Ambrosia calls me direct. "I love you, brother man. I truly, truly do. Thank you from the bottom of my heart."

I scream as loud as I can, for as long as I can.

The red woman is there in a white robe with a look of concern. I pull her into my arms, press my lips to hers and fill her mouth with my tongue. I taste her from lips to toes.

We fuck. We don't want to stop, ever.

The phone rings. We keep on fucking.

The sun rises and falls. We fuck.

"Kaden, would you like to be with me forever. This can be forever if you want it."

I look at her astonished that she even has to ask that question.

"What about Miyuki? What about your daughter growing toward birth? If you go with me forever, you will lose them forever."

Why is she doing this, this nagging? They will be better without me. My other two wives, my other two children, do better without me. Shit!

I answer by kissing her hard between her legs in her creamy, sweet spot. She makes it sweeter.

"And your screenplay, your script. Can you leave that behind? Can you abandon that?"

She is on top of me doing incredible things. I blink and lose my concentration. "What? What did you say?"

She works her hips like a magic massage. "To be with me, you have to leave all that here." She makes a twist that brings tears to my eyes.

"What I thought was we would be here. Where would we be?"

"In a better place. Just the two of us, forever."

She leans down and licks my lips.

I concentrate on what she is doing to my dick. We finish together and lay side by side staring up at the wood ceiling. I close my eyes and I see her breasts and vagina, taste them, need them. I have to have her again, now. But she sits up in the bed and crosses her legs and gives me that lighthouse smile.

"Kaden, you have been kind and generous to me. I don't want to take advantage of you. If you like you can stay here and enjoy your success, family, and friends."

She has my attention now. "And us? What about us?"

"I'm very busy, Kaden, but I will make time for us. I will do that to repay your kindness."

I reach for her to kiss her, but she holds me back. "If you want to do this, we should do it now. I want you very much, but you have to decide now."

"Why? What's the hurry? We..."

"Time is running out on us. Others are coming to interfere. We don't want that, do we?"

I shake my head no. "I want to be with you. This has been the best day of my life. I want to be with you."

She smiles that special smile I love to see. "Three days since you completed your screenplay."

"Three? No! No way. How..."

"I need your soul. Not this minute, not right now. You will have a long healthy life. I will collect your soul on the last day of your lush life with Miyuki and your children and grandchildren."

•

We are in our underwear. She is straddling me in the kitchen chair feeding me breakfast, rubbing her breasts against me, licking the grease from my lips.

Hurricane Rika arrives, blows open the door and bears down on us with deadly intent.

"I knew it was you! I just knew it. You lying piece of scarlet filth. You, you fucking cheating, lying red lump of defecation!"

At first, I thought Rika was screaming at me, but she is all up in the red woman's face, spraying spit and venom.

My new lover is cool, too cool, scary cool.

"Rika, your wrath is an old and tired act. Sit, Rika, enjoy the warmth of the last bridge you have to burn. Sit, now, before I lose my patience with you."

"Fuck you bitch!" Rika sits and pops right up. "Kaden, you stupid fuck, did you make a deal with it? Did you? Did you?"

I smile sheepishly. I shrug. "How do you know her…"

Rika cuts me off. "Her? Her? You mean Beelzebub? You mean Scratch? Fucking Lucifer? What did it promise you, Kaden?"

"Rika, it was just a joke. We were just joking around… right?"

My red woman slides off me, stands over me, looks at me tenderly. "Everything I promised and more is yours."

Rika collapses onto a chair shaking her head in disgust and despair.

Now I'm standing. "Come on. Come on. You, you… this is not real…"

"Kaden, you can call me Tyre. All I promised and more." Tyre holds out her hands to me. I step back from her. I look at Rika. Rika returns my look for a second and looks away. It is way too quiet in my writer's camp now. I hear an owl hoot near the cabin.

"Kaden, I'm sorry. I'm sorry. You did a deal for the screenplay. I never meant for you…"

"Rika, the screenplay is mine, by myself, honest. I didn't make a deal for the screenplay."

Tyre nods her concurrence and smiles at Rika.

"Poor Rika, poor baby — you underestimated your ex-lovers, colleagues, friends, and co-worker. That is an ongoing problem with you, Rika."

Rika ignores Tyre and stands facing me.

"For what? For what did you sell your soul? What did you want so fucking bad?"

I open my mouth and try to speak, but there is no sound.

Tyre has her arms around my waist.

"Tell her, Kaden. Tell the Brazilian-Swedish slut about our contract."

I swallow hard and croak out a response, "I get her. I get Tyre." I pull away from Tyre. "I... I..."

Rika is laughing now. Laughing and crying and snotting and sounding crazy. She stops at last. "Tyre is not a she or a he or male or female or boy or girl. Tyre is a fucking it. It! She fooled you and lied to me. Oh, fuck."

I turn to Tyre. "Are, are you..."

Tyre has turned away from me and is glaring at Rika. "Rika, twice you have accused me of lying to you. I never lied to you. I gave you what you asked for and more. I never lied to you, ever."

Rika whips out her cell phone. "You promised in red and white, in our blood, that I would be the top producer in Hollywood. The top dog, number one, with no one else even close. There!" Rika tosses the phone to me. I catch it and read the red lettering on white paper. "Read it, Kaden. Fucking read it."

"Sit down Rika. I will make this right if I lied to you." Tyre turns to me. "Kaden, sweet and kind Kaden, you be the judge. If you believe I lied. I will return Rika her soul. Is that fair, Rika?"

"Fuck you, Abaddon. I don't trust you at all."

"Of course you don't, but you trust Kaden. You just trusted him with your career, which is for you, the same as your poor miserable excuse for a life. What do you have to lose?"

Rika sits across from Tyre and stares at her for a moment. "If I win, you free both of us from your crooked soul stealing agreements."

Tyre leans toward Rika. "No. I will free one soul, but I will let you select which one, you or Kaden."

The two women sit across from each other at much at war as any two armies.

Rika sighs and she folds her hands in prayer. "Let Kaden go. He... he... let him go."

"Fuck that, Rika. Save yourself. You need to save yourself."

"Wow! This is wonderful it would appear that you two have some affection for each other. We will see how this works out. Kaden, would you please read our agreement out loud?"

"Within twelve months of this agreement, Rika Sandoval will be recognized by her peers, the press, and the public as the most powerful and influential producer in Hollywood. And Rika promises to deliver her soul to Tyre or her minions twenty-five years from the date of this agreement. — Are you guys serious? Are you two for real?"

Tyre turns to me with that irresistible smile. "Kaden, despite your continuing infatuation with this paranoid monster on steroids, was Rika number one as described in our contract?"

I turn to look at Rika. "You were, Rika. You were the boss of bosses."

Tyre smiles at Rika. "Yes, a king of kings."

"Fuck you both! She has you fucking enchanted. Kaden, what is my position in the industry today, right now?"

"You're not even in the business today. You are probably the most hated person in Hollywood."

"So much for your fucking contract. You fucking lied."

"Oh, I think not. Kaden, why is your friend so thoroughly detested by all those she has worked with?"

"The truth is that you treated us all like shit. You are petty, vindictive, arrogant, exploitative, and on a good day, just plain evil."

"Wow! Well put and heart felt. Kaden, in light of what you just said, do you believe I kept my part of our bargain?"

It takes me about thirty-seconds to consider Tyre's question. "I don't know if you helped her get to the top, but she was number one in the industry. From what I have seen she was the cause of her own downfall. Rika, as good as you were at climbing to the top you were better at falling into the pit."

Tyre is beaming like a red sun. "Rika, do you still want to save Kaden's soul or have you reconsidered?"

Rika is breathing deeply and staring at me with a look of confusion, anger and frustration. She starts to speak, but just shakes her head and flops back into her chair.

For the moment, there is just the sound of Rika's harsh breathing.

I turn to Tyre. "Did you help her get to the top?"

My answer is another beatific smile. "I was essential to her ascent, but I never lifted a finger to help her."

"I don't understand. How could you be essential if you never helped?"

The smile moves from me to Rika. "I told Rika she would succeed to the level she desired. She did the climb to the top on her own. Rika, you always had the raw talent, vicious cunning and ruthless drive. You just needed someone to free you up to do it."

There are tears rolling down Rika's cheeks as she sits with her head bowed.

"Tyre, did you cause her to... to self-destruct like that?"

"I was essential to her descent, but I never lifted a finger to harm her. Kaden, don't look so confused. Much of Rika's unfortunate behavior may be rooted in her ill-founded belief that I, not she, was the cause of her rise to fame and fortune."

Rika finally finds her voice again. "You motherfucker, you did nothing except play me like a fucking piano. You never lifted a fucking finger. You let me rise because you knew I would fucking fall. You dirty motherfucker."

"No hard feelings, Rika, please. You sought me out at the Crossroads. You begged me to help you. I declined, but you begged so sweetly and made such succulent promises and delivered such sweet favors I relented. And here we are."

"Fuck you, bitch. Just fuck you. You might as well take my soul now. God, how I fucked up."

"Wait, wait just a minute. Tyre, it wasn't just the soul you were after it was the show — The Rise and Fall of Rika Sandoval — you enjoyed the fucking show. You wrote the script for the show. You loved the fucking show!"

And now I get the smile and the laugh and the kiss and the tongue and the full body press.

"Oh, please, you two deserve each other. Oh, shit how stupid, dumb and fucking blind I..."

"Rika, shut up. Just shut up and listen." Rika gives us both the finger as she stands to leave. "Rika, sit the fuck down and hear me out. Like I heard you out. Just listen."

I put my hands on Tyre's shoulder. "Tyre, let's have act two. Rika has a great property, with a wonderful script, and... and if she can get back to number one, if she could do that would you give her back her soul? I mean what a show that would be and we could both watch it together. Now, that would be something."

46

Tyre's eyes are as bright as flames, her skin glows like an ember, her smile is blinding. That's our answer.

We all shake hands on it.

Rika hugs me goodbye before she leaves to start working on saving her soul. "Kaden, I suppose you want to cancel our agreement based on what you have learned about me, about what I am. I can understand if you do…"

That's not what I want to do. I spend the next few hours showing Tyre what I want to do, before I get back to my family and my life, if I ever can. I mean, how can I resist live theater on this intimate scale? A soul is a small price to pay for the best seats in the house.

Kaden, I thought I knew you, inside and out, but you do have the capacity to surprise and even shock me — may the devil take your eternal soul.

JC AND THE PROJECT KIDS

I met him. I did. At least, I think I did. I met him right here in our little, hot-as-hell Central Valley town. Just listen to me for a minute or two, and you tell me what you think.

So, like, I'm like, down on Railroad Avenue, a block from Willies' Wing joint when I see Fat Black yelling at some little nigger in a white linen suit, white straw stingy brim and sandals.

Fat was all upset and screaming. Fat was just about to go off on the little man. Shit, I felt sorry for the little guy, but we got our own peace keepers on Railroad Avenue — The Association would take care of that kinda shit better than I could.

I'm just about to ease on by Fat when he yells out my name and tells me to get my ass over there. I don't want to get into it with Fat, but maybe if he messing with me the little guy can get away.

When I get to them, Fat is practically foaming at the mouth.

"Tell him! Tell him! Hector tell him he can't go around doing that shit. You tell him."

I turn to the little guy. He's as brown as I am with a nose like a light bulb, brown eyes, and big working man's hands.

"You can't do that shit. Whatever that shit is. In fact, you need to get your ass out of here. It's almost closing time."

Fat is vindicated. He starts to calm down. I start to move on. Fat grabs my arm.

Fat turns back to the little man. "So tell me, you ain't gonna do that anymore. You tell me that now."

I hope the little nigger can take a hint. I shake Fat's hand off me.

"Niggers, it's been fun, but I gotta run. The wings are calling me."

The little guy speaks up. He has a nice voice deeper than expected, kinda familiar. "You going to get wings? Turkey wings?"

Short stuff turns back to Fat. "Look, if nobody asks, I won't tell. How about that?"

This works for me. "Shit, sounds good to me. Let's go get some wings."

That's not good enough for Fat. "No! Don't say that again ever. You might end up like him sooner than you think."

Fat is adamant. His patience is just about gone and mine is beginning to ebb too.

"Fat turns to me. You know what he said, right?"

Of course, I've no idea what they're arguing about, but I see The Association Peace Keepers headed directly toward us. "Fat, he from out of town. Look at him, man, he don't know how things is here."

I'm about to jet when The Peace Keepers suddenly turn and start running away from us toward Grand Street.

I turn to shake hands with the little nigger and pull him away from Fat at the same time.

There's a brilliant flash like a flare just went off in my head. I end up flat on my ass on the sidewalk leaning against a wire fence.

For a moment, I'm blinded. When I can finally see, I see the little guy is fanning me with his hat. He looks worried. I'm not worried. I'm mad as hell.

"Jesus Christ, what the hell was that?"

Suddenly, Fat is roaring in my face, "He ain't Jesus Christ, Owen! He ain't. He just think he is."

I slowly turn to Fat, "What the fuck have you got me into?"

"He ain't Jesus, man. You know that. I know that. Shit. That's what I been trying to tell you, Owen. He ain't Jesus."

I guess Fat was going to prove his point by tossing the little man down the road a few hundred feet. Fat barely touches the little man and he's sitting on the sidewalk beside me. He's blinking and waving his hands around like he's blind.

I sit there on the ground knocked down by something I don't understand, by a little nigger I could sweep the floor with, with one hand.

Right then and there, I decide I'm going to kill Fat. I'm going to beat him to death. He done drug me into some shit that's way over my head. I've a very bad feeling about this.

Fat kinda senses something is going to come down. He tries to scramble to his feet, stumbles and falls. He tries to crawl away. Don't matter to me. He's one dead nigger. I never liked him that much anyway.

I come to my feet easy, in one smooth motion and the little guy's right there in front of me, blocking me. He's different somehow, maybe not so small. His eyes are different too: hard, hard as diamonds.

We lock eyes for a moment.

"The wings are on me, Hector."

His voice is different too — something in there is raw, mean and steely.

I look back at the little guy. I look him up and down.

"Who the fuck are you?"

"We can talk about it over wings, OK?"

We get a twenty piece party bucket and bottles of water. I end up paying. All the little deadbeat had was euros and Willie ain't taking no funny money.

We walk up to Willow Creek Park and sit at a picnic table under the moon light.

The wings is special — Willie got them right again — for a while there he was off his game. The little man's loving them too.

"Hey, if you is who you say you is. Why did you zap us? You coulda warned us. I mean, you know all and see all, right?"

"Who told you that?"

"You did, in the Bible."

"I didn't write any Bibles."

"No, no but your boys, crew... I mean disciples..."

"I don't write books. I don't even read that much. I prefer movies and some television."

I'm at a loss for words. I just watch him rip into those turkey wings.

"Ahhh, OK. Well, you must have read the Bible at least once, right? I mean, you know the Bible, right?"

"Hector, there are too many versions. I tried honest man, but I didn't like what was being said about me. I never finished one. How do they end?"

Now I got a little headache.

"You want me to tell you how the Bible ends?"

"If you don't mind."

"How far did you get into the... your Bible?"

"Not very far. Hey, you falling behind on these wings."

"What page did you stop on?"

"I truly don't remember."

"But you know everything, see everything."

"See, that's exactly why I don't read the Bibles, way too much exaggeration and outright, shameless misrepresentations. Come on, Hector, I'm not the CIA."

"Wow! All those kids going to Sunday school and all those folks studying the Bible... Bibles, and you ask me how it ends. Wow!"

"Bibles, Hector, a lot of different Bibles."

I'm really stumped as to what to say to the wing-eating little nigger. In fact, I'm scared to ask him anything.

I see the three boys coming up the path toward us about the same time they see us. Two good-sized boys walking like they been around and one skinny little fool in front like he leading a parade. Now that ain't right. Why are the streetwise kids letting the punk lead?

"What do you think they want?"

The boys are coming up behind little nigger — no way he could have seen them. I ain't surprised and don't ask no questions. I'm clean out of questions for Little Man.

"They into mischief. Hey, I'm gonna let you handle this. Zap em like you did me and Fat Black."

The boys saunter up to the table. Skinny does the talking.

"What you faggots doing out here? This is our park, motherfuckers."

Little Man holds out the wing bucket to the boys. "You're welcome to share. They're excellent."

"Faggot, we want your fucking money. We buy our own wings. And you better have some long green, cause we way hungry."

Skinny boy lifts his t-shirt to show us his pistol. So that's why he's the leader. The streetwise boys know that this is not going right — we should at least be showing a little concern. They exchange looks. I reach for another wing.

Skinny's starting to realize the shit's not right, but he doesn't know what to do next.

At last, skinny pulls out his old thirty-eight revolver and he points it at me.

"Give me your fucking wallet."

"Skinny, you got to deal with him." I nod toward my Lord and hopefully, Savior. "That's *The Man*. You deal with him."

"Roscoe, you are supposed to be home watching your sister like you promised your mother. You need to go do that." As Little Man speaks, he glances at Roscoe.

Roscoe, the bigger of the big boys, don't say shit. He just holds up his hands indicating he wants no part of this action anymore. He backs up quick and a moment later, he's a streak in the wind.

"Walter," Little Man is talking to the other big boy, "you got fifteen minutes to beat your probation officer to your house."

Walter starts to respond to Little Man, but Little Man gives him that look. The boy sprints like a track star on his way out of the park.

"Hector, I'm falling behind you here. That one's yours." He nods toward skinny.

Skinny is thoroughly confused. He still has his gun, but it's pointed down at the grass.

"How did, did you know, know their names and, and stuff?"

I look skinny up and down. "Po-Po. You don't even know Five-O when you see him. Go on home, boy."

"Five-O. He's Five-O?"

"Fool, he knows everyone on probation or parole. Don't believe me? Ask Roscoe or Walter if you can catch them."

Skinny's a little slow, but he's starting to understand that there's some weird shit going down. He starts to back away.

"Oh, and throw that gun in the lake as you go."

Skinny finally got it. He stutters, "Yes, sir," to Little Man's command or is it a Commandment?

He tosses the pistol as far as he can out into the lake and scares the shit out of some sleeping ducks.

Little Man wipes his mouth, shakes his head in pure delight. "Hector, thanks, man, I owe you one. Hey, could I ask you a question; no, could I ask you two questions?"

I look him straight in the eyes. He looks damn serious. I wonder if this is going to be a Saint Peter interview and the wrong answers will doom me for all eternity. What the fuck? I'm doomed anyway.

"Ask away."

"Now, Fat Black's a Negro, or African American, or Afro-American, or colored, or mulatto, even I can see that — but he's as white as a virgin snowfall and as skinny as a rail, so why do you call him Fat Black? I don't understand that."

I'm dumbfounded. I don't understand this dude at all. My mouth is moving, but no words are coming out.

"Hector, are you OK?"

Of course I'm not OK. I may never be OK again.

"OK, I just wasn't expecting that question." I pause a minute to collect my memories. "Melvin and Grant, that's Fat Black to you, and I was chilling on the back porch of my unit in the project. We was eight or nine I think. Some of the little kids was shooting marbles nearby. Grant says something about how dark Melvin's mother is. Melvin tells Grant his skinny pale ass is just a fat-black-wannabe. It wasn't that funny, but it made me laugh. And the little kids started laughing and calling Grant 'Fat Black.' Grant got pissed and swung on Melvin and missed. Of course, the little kids laughed at that, too. At that point, it would have all ended right there, but Grant turned on the little kids taunting him. That was a bad move. He caught Jimmy Brown or one of the other little kids and started shaking him. Melvin and I had to step in. The little kids got their revenge. They spread the word and pretty soon everyone was calling Grant 'Fat Black.' By the end of elementary school, a lot of kids thought 'Fat Black' was his real name."

Little Man has stopped eating wings. He's thinking real hard on what I said. I don't know why.

Now I've a question, "Hey — prayers — do you answer prayers? What happens to prayers?"

"Thank you, Hector, I've one more question."

"What about prayers?"

"Sure, I will explain prayers to you, but just answer my other question first. It's really important to me."

I look at him a minute. I hope this question is more serious than the last one. On second thought, the less serious, the better.

"I know your name is Owen, so why do they call you Hector?"

My mind was going numb. At that point, I was thinking maybe I should withdraw the question about prayers. I'm pretty sure I'm not going to like the answer."

"That's your question? Really?"

Little Man nods yes.

"I was fourteen or fifteen. I had the hots for Gloria Henry. The problem was that her brother was the baddest dude in the projects. John Henry took over the projects' drug trade for all three buildings by the time he was twenty-one. The things he cared most about in the world was his grandmother who raised him and his sister, Gloria.

I was over at the Dos Rios Projects where the Henrys lived. It was me, Melvin, Spider, and Fat Black. We was a few stoops down from John Henry's stoop. John Henry was sitting on the top step, and his three lieutenants were sitting on the steps below. All of them looking straight ahead as John Henry gave them their instructions.

After his crew left, Gloria came and sat by her brother. This is why I was over here. I wanted a chance to see and maybe even talk to Gloria. I couldn't do that with John Henry there. He had made it real clear what he would do to anyone messing with his sister.

As it was, Gloria didn't even look down our way.

After a few minutes, the phone rang in John Henry's unit. He went in to answer it and Gloria was outside alone.

Fat Black started the shit. He pulled out a ten dollar bill and told me it was mine if I went up there and kissed Gloria. Even then, Fat Black was in 'The Game.' The last time I had a ten dollars of my own was two birthdays ago.

Spider said he would be a lookout for a dollar.

Melvin pulled out a dollar and said he would pay the lookout fee if I did it.

Shit, that was an irresistible temptation, big money and a hot woman.

I took a deep breath and sprinted up to Gloria. She heard me running and turned toward me just in time for me plant a big one right on her lips.

She squealed in delight and surprise. She put her arms around my neck and was kissing me when John Henry bolted out the door and leaped down the steps.

I had maybe two steps on him. I could hear him breathing like a mad bull and shaking the ground like a freight train. I ran for my life. I ran faster than I could possibly run. I was running on spirit and will power, and that big nigger was still right on my ass. I ran all the way around his project building, and still he wouldn't quit.

I heard, in the far distance, people yelling and screaming. I didn't understand what they were saying.

On the second lap, John Henry started losing ground. By the time, we got back to his stoop the nigger was about to collapse. I looked back and saw him stagger to a stop. He was barely standing, swaying and gasping. He bent over with his hands on his knees. A strong breeze would knock his ass over.

If I had stopped right there, it would have all worked out. I would have been a project hero for running the mighty John Henry into the ground. My name would still ring out today as a legendary hero like David from David and Goliath. You know who they are, right? I mean, I had kissed Gloria for only the second time. I had ten dollars. And I had vanquished the baddest nigger in the projects. Oh, I was going to get an ass whipping eventually, I knew that, but that would have made me an even bigger hero.

My mother said my big problem was I didn't have stopping sense. She may have been on to something. I walked back to John Henry and stood in front of him. He was too weak to even glare at me.

I looked around at all the people hanging out their windows and standing on their stoops — all the kids who were following our great race, Gloria standing in suspense — all of them looking at me.

I took my right index finger and pushed John Henry over. He fell like a redwood tree.

All of a sudden, everything went quiet. It was like all the air was sucked out of the world. Everything froze in time and space. And I knew, as much as I know anything in this life that I had fucked up, fucked-up big time.

John Henry hit the ground for about two seconds, and he bounced up like a jack-in-the-box. He came up swinging. I hit the ground with the first blow. I didn't bounce up, I covered up.

He was still weak, and his punches were at a quarter of normal, but he was killing me.

Normally, someone would have stepped in to keep a man from beating a child to death like that. I think most of the people thought this was a lesson I had coming. I earned this beating, with interest.

What saved my black ass was my sister, Magda. She was visiting friends and heard the commotion. When she figured out who was getting beat she snatched up a garbage can lid and a garden trowel. She charged John Henry and knocked him off me with her garbage can shield. She stood over him daring him to lay a hand on me.

Magda was seventeen or eighteen, but she was for real. Our big sister's always for real.

John Henry looked up and saw Magda looming over him with that shield and little shovel, I think he fell in love on the spot. End of story."

Little Man is smiling. I think he might even laugh.

"You have led an exciting life. Still, how did you get the name Hector from these events?"

"A lot of kids in the projects spent the summer reading. Whole tribes of us would go off to the downtown library every week to return and get library books.

If one kid found something interesting that interest would spread like a plague. That summer it was Greek and Roman mythology. Get it?"

Now he's laughing, it's a huge ass laugh that shakes the trees like a stormy wind. Tears are rolling out of his eyes. I really don't think it's that funny.

"Hector, brave Hector at Troy, challenges mighty Hercules. Hercules chases him around the city walls and slays poor heroic and foolish Hector, very apt. Who first saw the similarities between the two events?"

"Shit, Melvin and Spider at first, I think, but everybody agreed it was right on. Everybody saw it, I guess, even my mother."

We sit there for moment. I have to laugh. I do. We laugh together for a while, but I don't think we're laughing at the same thing. I'm laughing at this little nappy-headed fool claiming to be, you know who, and he know more about Greek and Roman mythology than he know about the Bible or Bibles.

After that, we shake hands, no shock at all, and he's off up toward Broadway.

I don't know how this is going to turn out. I don't even know who or what Little Man is. I just know that I can't avoid him. I know that would be as wrong as pushing John Henry over. I got to face up to him, whatever the consequence.

But you know what really worries me and keeps worrying me? And, I ain't told anybody this, but Little Man told me to leave Fat Black alone. Fat Black didn't get me into this mess. Little Man said he was waiting for me all along. He wouldn't say why. He said he would explain it all to me when he came back.

You know what? I can wait. Shit, I can wait forever. I hope Little Man is gone for a long, long time. If I see him on my deathbed, it would be too soon. I was here for the second coming, I sure as hell don't want to be here for the third coming. I do believe he might be coming just for me. I really believe that.

SNIPER

The New Springfield 7.62×51mm sniper, SO, with inversion scope, has perfect balance, elegantly carved walnut stocks, precision parts, outstanding reliability and incredible accuracy. It fits hands, shoulder, face and eyes like an extension of the body. It's an exceptionally fine tool for killing people at long range.

It is not a crew weapon. The inversion scope eliminates the need for a spotter. The gun is a work of art. It is one of the finest tools I have ever had the pleasure of operating, but just for four months and twenty-five days.

The replacement is a hunk of junk. Plastic, carbon fiber, chemistry set materials, unnatural and unreal, without personality or appeal.

If the Lieutenant or the Captain or even the Major had tried to get me to trade my New Springfield for that Star Wars bullshit, we would have exchanged words. I would have kept my Springfield, turned my back, walked away and that would have been the end of it.

But the "Bowling Ball," the Chief Master Sergeant, came for my gun. His black-bowling-ball bald head with a neck-less attachment to his bowling ball torso and his bowling ball fist rolled up on me pointed at my Springfield and placed a plastic gun case on my bunk.

Not one word out of him. I should have told him to fuck off, to get lost. I should have stared him down. I should have... I swallowed hard, shook my head and handed him that prized extension of me.

As he departed with my rifle, he said, "Three days." I interpreted this to mean that if I was still unhappy in three days, I could come and see him and he would return my weapon of choice. I hope that's what he meant.

The plastic toy replacement has poor weight distribution, worse balance, feels cheap and is as ugly as homemade sin. It is infused with hideous green-gray camouflage colors and infected with odd bumps, grooves, indentations and rough, unfinished spots. It's a fucking disaster.

There is no scope. There is a tiny screen that pops up where the scope should be. There are three circles that the shooter is supposed to line up on the target. Three cameras in the make-believe gun supply the images on the screen. It is fucking ridiculous.

There is a sixteen-hour training video that comes with this Frankenstein of a weapon. I watch the first three minutes. What a fucking waste.

•

I have targets one mile out and moving on foot, three armed males well-spaced and keeping low with good intermittent cover. Impossible shots. The plastic feels so alien against my skin, and I'm uncomfortable with the balance of the weapon; the screen is way too small, and... I stop thinking. I breathe life into the plastic, sweat feeling into the unfeeling, ground the butt of the weapon into the flesh and blood of my shoulder. I line up the circles. The gun fires me. The gun pulls my trigger finger.

"Control, this is Alpha Hotel, off targets, three down. Mission accomplished. I'm homeward bound."

•

I take the rifle in for a calibration check. I have to do this every day for the first week of use. The techie shines a little flashlight at the gun as I enter the tech shop.

"What did you just do with that gadget?"

The techie holds up the tiny tube for my inspection. "I turned it off. This is a remote on/off."

"Well, shit. I should have one of those."

"You need to take that up with the brass or God or somebody, but not me."

•

On the second day of calibration, I have a complaint. "See look at the counter. It shows one shot fired and three killed. It should be one for one."

The same techie pulls up the screen, and we watch a playback of my last shot. There is one shot that kills three targets. Wow!

"Come on, hotshot, you need to watch the movies after the kills."

I don't watch the movies, ever.

•

On the third day of calibration, I'm just opening the door to leave when the techie calls me back. "Hotshot, come on back. It checks out. Take your rifle. I don't need to see you or your weapon again. Good-bye and good luck."

•

I don't use the circles or the screen anymore. I pick her up, hold her tight, close my eyes — she shoots me. The movies go to headquarters on some wireless connection. I get letters of commendation.

•

Two weeks after she comes into my life. I pass the Bowling Ball. He stops talking on his Com/Phone long enough to say, "Henderson, for God's sake, don't fall in love with the bitch."

I have a smart-ass answer on the tip of my tongue, but the Bowling Ball has moved on and it's too late… I mean… I mean it's too late to respond to the Chief Master Sergeant. That's what I mean.

ALBINO

I favor the alleys. I stroll the alleys home from my nights out at the club or at her or his place. Alleys fit me. I find things in the alleys. Sometimes things find me in the alleys, things like *the voice*.

The voice is raspy, harsh, angry, evil, lusty, sexy, odd and uneven. Stops me in my tracks, tilts my head to hear better, sobers me to appreciate better. That voice makes me sweat, my fingers tingle, my dick throb.

I follow it to an illegal club in the alley. I give the doorman some bills, step from the dank, dark alley into the dismal, dark club.

All eyes are on her. Her is in a silver tight, sparkly gown painted on a thin frame with a sweet apple of an ass. Her is a black woman with full lips, well-rounded nose and crinkly blonde hair.

Her is paler than her dress. Her is white. Her is an albino wearing dark glasses and singing to me, staring at me.

"Down in the valley
Deep in the cut
Backs bow
Bodies bend
Stuff flows
Skin glows
Yours and mine
Down in the valley

Deep in the cut"

She glues me to the floor, leaves me wanting more of her music and all of her. She whispers in that voice just to me.

"I'll shuck you like corn
Shell you like peas
Peel you to the core
Skin you alive
Stuff you with
Garlic and cloves
Bury you deep
Wear your skin home
Go home in your skin
In your skin
In your skin"

And she's gone, left everybody in a trance. The applause is hesitant and a little nervous, leaves folks blinking and looking around to make sure they are where they're supposed to be.

I start to the back in the direction she disappeared and someone taps me on the shoulder. I turn and there she is with a little black leather jacket over her gown.

I reach out and touch her face. "You are the alabaster Shakespeare wrote of and the always new snow and the color of eternity."

She touches my face and — in that voice that is as soft now and, somehow, edgier – she leans in and whispers in my ear, "I'm the color of death and old bleached bones and eternal loss, but that just makes you need me more and more and more." The tip of her tongue touches my ear as she speaks, sparks my need into a nova.

I kiss her, tongue her, grind her, handle her ass with rough affection and trade her a whisper. "Your voice had me before I ever saw you. Your looks are just the cream in my coffee."

She laughs and laughs and leads me out the door.

"You would fuck my voice, fondle my vowels, consume my consonants, and admire my adjectives?"

Down the alley, we go.

"I would do that to every aspect of your body and soul."

We cut cross Main Street into another alley.

"Will you take me home to meet your mother after we fuck?"

"I think you have fucking on your mind."

So we do it in the alley up against the wall.

She smiles and laughs. "You are very much in lust with a voice and a color and a body, I think."

We are in the lobby of an old shabby apartment building.

I send a text as she unlocks her door. I hand her my phone as I unzip her gown.

She reads the message out loud, "Moms, I have found her. I will bring her for Sunday dinner."

She laughs me into her bed, body and soul.

I awake to the smell of perking coffee and frying eggs and ham. She appears in the doorway in a short thin red robe that accents her familiar looking, deep-brown skin with red undertones, so much like mine and not like the porcelain hand that that I'm pointing at her.

I speak in a raspy, harsh, angry, evil, lusty, sexy, odd and uneven voice. "Fuck you! Dinner is off! My mother would not recognize me, her own son. For God's sake, what did you do?"

She gives me a lazy smile

"Son? Are you sure?"

I will not look under the sheet. Nothing can make me look under the fucking sheet. Nothing! As she turns to leave, there is the flash of a penis in his open gown.

A ROAMING TAT

This is without a shadow of a doubt the most disgusting pigsty of a tattoo shop I have ever had the displeasure of visiting. It's in the bathroom of an abandoned Shell station about ten miles off Highway 99, just south of Fresno. It reeks of urine and feces and is littered with used condoms and soiled sanitary napkins.

The walls are smeared with what looks like dried feces graffiti. I hold my breath as I address the two thin, bearded white men in immaculate white doctor jackets with name tags reading, "Alphonse" and "Dupree." Despite the jackets, they're somewhat lacking in bedside manner.

"What the fuck you want?" asks Dupree, angry at the first sight of me.

"How did you find us? Who told you about us?" snarls Alphonse as he reaches under his jacket and pulls out a silver revolver.

Mindy, Joe, and Albert all told me this was a bad idea, but I didn't listen to them. Now I wish I had. I hold up my hands as I back out of the doorway.

"Sorry, sorry. I was looking for a tat, a… a special tat. And… ahh… someone told me that you two did, did special tats."

My mouth is dry, and my underarms are compensating by creating a river of sweat.

"Get the fuck out of here!" Alphonse seems serious as he points his pistol at me.

"You're too fucking dark for a decent tat. You need to leave that to us Aryans," says a sneering Dupree.

I take one more step back. "You may be right. I mean, that makes sense, yes. Sorry to have bothered you." Now, twenty steps to my car and a very fast exit.

I'm halfway to my car when one of them yells, "Stop! Stop right there. I be a little curious about you, about what you're really up to. What tat was you looking for?"

"You be quick and careful now, boy. Why you here?" coming from the other one.

I turn back to face them, "I'm looking for a roaming tat."

Alphonse steps out the door now and aims the pistol at me, "Nigger, you better make sense quick."

I blink the sweat out of my eyes and summon rusty words through my dry mouth, "A roaming tat. A tat that moves around on your body, moves from place to place."

Alphonse is there in an instant with the barrel of his revolver against my forehead, "Nigger, somebody playing a trick on your black ass or are, are you trying to play us for the fool?"

I swallow hard and concentrate on getting my tongue, lips and mouth to coordinate an understandable response, "I... I saw one. I saw one in the PI. In the Phil—"

"In the Philippines? You lying sack of shit!" Dupree is so close he is spitting in my face, "Tats don't move, you dumb motherfucker."

"Wait, wait... describe it," there's a change in Alphonse's voice that catches Dupree's and my attention.

Alphonse's eyes are wider, and he's lessened the gun's pressure against my skull.

"I was in a whore house playing cards with two Navy guys and a Marine. The Marine had an old buffalo nickel tat on the back of both wrists. The buffalo was on the nickel on the right wrist, and the nickel was on the left wrist but without the buffalo."

"Bull buffalo shit! I..."

Alphonse cuts Dupree off with dangerous intensity, "You shut the fuck up."

Dupree starts to say something, but Alphonse has aimed his revolver at his doctor partner. Dupree is the one sweating and looking anxious now.

Alphonse nods for me to continue.

"I asked the Marine about it and he bet me a dollar that within an hour the buffalo would move from the right wrist to the left wrist. I took that bet. The Navy guys wanted some of that and so they bet the farm."

"And the buffalo moved up his arm across his collar bones and down to the nickel on his left wrist."

I'm fucking astonished at Alphonse's words. We just look at each other for a minute.

Alphonse lowers his gun and steps back from me, "Don't look for that tat master. Leave it alone." He turns and walks away.

I leave with prayers of thanks and lots of questions about Alphonse and his warning.

●

"Warren, you are so seriously fucked up. Why this fascination, no, this obsession with a tattoo. You are forty-years old and you never wanted a tattoo before or a piercing, not even your ears."

Mindy, my girlfriend of ten years and mother of Joy, our five-year-old daughter, and I are sitting on the floor of our apartment as Mindy effortlessly rolls a slender joint.

"Mindy, I'm trying…"

"And what is this tattoo? Why won't you even tell me that?"

I understand her brown-eyed frustration. I'm not even sure why I'm pursuing this madcap, impossible solution.

She gives me the cross-eyed leer that always brings at least a smile to my face — but not this time. This time I lean over and kiss her, pull her to me and hold her tight.

I tell her the story I told the two shit-house tattoo artists and then I tell her the rest.

●

The Navy Petty Officers were furious at their losses. The club was full of Navy, and the Gunnery Sergeant was the only Marine I saw in the place.

My three Air Force buddies came to the table just as things appeared to reach a boiling point. I nodded to the jarhead to come with us. That would at least give the gunney better odds. I didn't like Marines or NCO's back

65

then — I still don't — but I like to see an individual have at least a fighting chance. The sergeant looked up at me with eyes as gray and cold as Thule fog. I took a step back and he picked up the dollar he had won from me and shoved it into my pocket.

"Hang on to this, flyboy. One day this tattoo will save your life."

He turned that barren, lost look on each of the Petty Officers. The two Navy NCO's reconsidered whatever they had on their minds and retired to the bar without another word.

●

"Warren, what are you trying to say?"

I kiss her again, stand and go retrieve a letter from my dresser drawer. I look in on Joy sleeping with her stuffed Big Bird. I watch her for a few soft minutes before I return to Mindy and hand her the letter. As she reads her hand trembles and she grows pale.

"Dear Mr. Alexander, per our discussion you have stage 4 lymph node cancer with widespread metastasis to lymph nodes, liver, and kidneys. As we discussed, your disease has advanced beyond the stage that surgical, radiation, or chemo treatment would be helpful."

Mindy does not cry or moan and we talk well into the morning. She does not agree with my last ditch, wild-shot, desperation gamble — she would rather the three of us celebrate our last days together enjoying each other and engaging in our favorite activities. In the end, I agree and stop looking for a magic tattoo solution.

●

The magic tattoo solution finds me in Anaheim while visiting Disneyland. I walk into the hotel barbershop, deserted except for one black barber motioning me to his chair.

I sit and he hands me his cellphone, "Please make a selection."

I think he is giving me pictures of hair styles, but when I look at the phone I see the buffalo nickel tattoos from long ago. I swipe the phone and there's a fighter jet on a black runway and the same runway but empty. I swipe again and again. There's a rabbit peeking out of a hole in the ground and the same hole empty. There is a bright colored, red and orange, elegantly-feathered bird sitting on her nest and then her empty nest. I stop after the first dozen.

I have a million questions, but I ask the most important one first, "Will it keep me alive?"

"Yes, far beyond the normal human lifetime."

"What does it cost? I mean, am I selling my soul?"

The brother looks bored with the whole process, "You have no monetary or service obligation to us and we have no interest in your soul. Someone prepaid for you long ago. The whole tattoo process takes sixty minutes and there's moderate pain during the tattoo."

I choose the colorful bird.

"I have to inform you that if you get these tattoos, if you get this significant life extension, you will not be able to commit suicide. We will not let you throw away the life extension we gave you. Do you understand this?"

I don't understand. This whole process is beyond my understanding. I want to live. I want to see Joy grow up and Mindy and I grow old together.

The barber hands me a thin densely printed brochure, "Please read this carefully and come back tomorrow if you still want the tattoos."

I glance at the pamphlet written in thick, impenetrable legalese.

"If possible, I would like to get this done now."

"Are you sure?"

Sixty minutes later I have my tattoo.

I leave with the sinking sensation that I have made a fool of myself all in vain.

●

Mindy is not happy with the tattoos, but she understands my extreme anxiety.

Joy is delighted with the bright bird on my wrist.

●

The next morning Mindy and Joy are off to breakfast as I sleep in. I'm on the toilet when the room phone starts ringing. I'm looking through the barber's pamphlet when a paragraph catches my eye.

"The recipient's life is extended by the life expectancy of the person having the greatest life expectancy to offer the recipient. We always select the life donor that has the closest ties to the recipient."

There's a banging on the door to our room. Someone's yelling through the door but I can only pick out the words, "Your daughter... Very serious... Come quickly."

HOME

I live up off Sorrel Creek road in Gusty Hills. Its eighty acres of good pasture land on rolling hills with majestic Blue Oaks and plebian scrub brush residing on gentle swells like green clad bosoms in the spring and tanned brown breasts in the fall.

I live in the house that my grandfather, father, and I were born in. A solid oak and sugar pine structure with redwood shingles and two stone fireplaces.

The wind up here is a sprightly daytime imp and a voracious nocturnal creature. It rouses at dusk and shakes the grass and rattles the oaks. That hardy breeze creaks my old house, making it moan and groan in wooden ecstasy.

I grew up being rocked by that wind and listening to her play the creaking wood and screeching nails of our stout home. Indeed, I sleep best when the wind freshens, finds her full voice and rules the hills, plucks the creek waters, flattens the grasses and bends the limbs of the great oaks to her will. I sleep like a baby, like the dead.

The land is all leased out now for horses, cattle, sheep and even goats.

●

I work in the city at jobs that put food on the table and helps pay the taxes on the land. The jobs are a necessary evil.

In the office, she is swinging her hips and — being full and ready to blush, blossom and bloom — she caught my eye. She ran a soft, steel hook through that eye and down through my guts to my gonads.

Her presence turned a necessary evil into a daily delight.

And, eventually, into lusty nights of moans, screams, secretions and sweet, sweet repose.

•

"Up here... up here you're so different... just... like..."

"Like what? How do you mean?"

We're sitting on my porch steps watching the sun bid us a fair thee well and a goodnight.

She closes her twin brown orbs under sun-tinted eyelids. She reaches for my hand.

"You walk these hills and just fade into them, blend... the wind and you... you belong... you disappear... merge with it all."

The breeze comforts her, soothes her cheeks and fluffs her curls with affection.

•

"Wake up! Wake up! There is someone out there, outside, on the porch, at the door."

She's pulling my shoulder, her short nails digging into my skin. I drag myself from deep sleep, give her a brief hug and move off into the dark room. I don't need a light, my feet know the way.

I take a kitchen chair and wedge it under the front doorknob. I do the same for the back door. I close and lock all the windows. The keys for the doors were lost in my grandfather's time, I don't ever remember locking the doors.

I try to sit with her and calm her, hold her and reassure her, but sleep, irresistible sleep dragged me back into its dark domain.

In the morning, we buy and install high-quality locks, deadbolts on the doors and new window locks. She's good with her hands and handy with tools.

We lunch outside on a blanket under an oak tree. She falls asleep with her head in my lap.

•

She's starting to show just a little mound like the hills in summer, gentle and brown.

•

"Where's your family pictures? I found ten pictures and three of those were of you and only one picture each of your mother and grandmother. Why is that? That is so odd."

She's sitting on the floor, eating a tub of Butter Brickle ice cream and sorting old documents and our paltry few photos.

"I don't know. That is odd. I remember old photo albums when I was a boy... three or four of them..."

•

At the breakfast table, she reads the newspaper article to me: "The victim was hit crossing the interstate on the Gusty Hills section. He has been identified as Rally Hastings, thirty-nine, of Bellflower, California. Mr. Hastings was wanted on outstanding warrants in Los Angeles and San Joaquin counties. Witnesses say Mr. Hastings appeared to be fleeing at the time of the accident, but they saw nothing threatening and no one other than other drivers were in the area."

"That was two nights ago when you heard someone on the porch, right?"

"Do you think it was him? Do you think it was Hastings?"

"It could have been. We rarely get visitors here. The house is not visible from the interstate or the county road. I think that's why we never bothered with locking the doors."

She looks at me, looks at me oddly.

I lean over and lick her milk mustache, and one thing leads to another.

•

"A midwife? Really? Why?"

We are in my old room putting together a Swedish handmade crib.

"Well, a doctor is fine if we can find one. My grandfather, father, and I were born in this house. I would like to keep the tradition going—"

"This is a lonely place. There're no close neighbors. The phone reception is poor at best. This place is kind of its own time zone."

"You don't want to live here? I thought you were getting used to the house and … sleeping better."

"It tolerates me and patronizes me: the house, the land, the wind, even the sky. I'm on a visa here in your land. I could never live here, never."

We sit across from each other silently, pleading and searching for some common ground.

"I could try to live in the city or in San Juan. We could…"

The look on her face says she doesn't believe me. I don't even believe me.

●

It is a smooth, and as she said "relatively easy delivery," of a seven pound and eight ounce boy with outstanding lungs and an appetite to match.

He sleeps between us that first night, and she asks, "Can we, our baby and I, leave here? Can we leave you or will I have an accident on the highway while you sleep?"

I answer as best I can. "You can come and go at will. You're always welcome here."

"And our baby?"

"Like me, like my father and grandfather, we can't live anywhere else. I don't think we can." I touch her cheek. "I know we can't."

I think at that moment that she will kill me in my sleep with her sturdy hands, steal away with our son or both. And it will change little or nothing. Dead or alive I will be home where I belong, and sooner, rather than later, she will have to bring him home to all of us. We will endure here at home as long as there is the wind, the water and the hills

ACKNOWLEDGMENTS

I must, first of all, acknowledge my wife, Ruth's, encouragement and support in my pursuing this time-consuming craft. I thank you for your patience and understanding.

Our daughter's Zenobia and Zora have taken time from their busy lives to respond to my request for comments on my work. I appreciate your time and insights. Our son-in-law, Thomas, has been an insightful reader and a timely responder.

Our grandson, Kenneth, has been an avid reader and promoter of my stories.

From my very first story my granddaughter, Roze has been my most excellent proofer and critic at large. Thank you again for all your help with and interest in my writing.

Dr. Travis Silcox at Sacramento City College introduced me to the art of writing short stories and encouraged me to publish and polish my craft. I'm forever in your debt.

Mr. Mensah Demary published my first two stories in "Specter Magazine," and steered me to tools that have helped me expand my publishing opportunities. Your support has been invaluable.

Dr. David Covin gave consistent encouragement and published my first collection of short stories.

My MeetUp group, Sacramento Prose and Poetry, is my sounding board and a major part of my writing community. I thank all the members of SPP, including but not limited to: Kae Sable, Elaine Zentner, Regnal Otto, Doug Huse, Jack Ratliff, Julie Howard, Lee Caldarella-Wong, Gary Stream, Patricia Wentzel, and our talented and gracious former leader Sara Winston.

My special editors, Chez Colson and Enaj Leotaud, who made every editing session a laughing matter.

I owe profound gratitude and countless thanks to my 2015 Callaloo workshop leaders, Ravi Howard and Jacinda Townson, for their expertise and patience.

I also must acknowledge all the fellow students, family, fellow writers, and friends too numerous to name who encouraged and inspired me.

Finally, and with great appreciation, I thank my editors at Choose the Sword Press: Damon Banner and especially Moriah Pearson for her expertise and fortitude in making this book a reality.

PREVIOUS PUBLICATIONS

"I Saw the Devil" - Specter Magazine
"Nina" - Piker Press
"Trinity" - Piker Press
"Bone Yard" - The Birds We Piled Loosely
"Wind Song" - Short Fiction Break
"Rocket Eighty-Eight Blues" - Sirenzine
"Crossroads" - The Fable Online
"Out of Order" - so glad is my heart.
"Albino" - Across the Margin
"Home" - Literally Stories
"A Roaming Tat" - Literally Stories
"Sniper" - CMC Review
"Diogenes" - Freedom Fiction Press

Frederick K. Foote, Jr. was born in Sacramento, California and educated in Vienna, Virginia, and Northern California. He started writing short stories and poetry in 2013.

He has published over eighty stories and poems including literary, science fiction, fables, and horror genres. A collection of his short stories, *For the Sake of Soul*, was published in October 2015 by Blue Nile Press.

A complete list of his publications can be found at fkfoote.wordpress.com